The Weeping Prince & The Mansion in Sand

Alice VL – Zandri Burger

The Weeping Prince & The Mansion in Sand

The Weeping Prince & The Mansion in Sand

Alice VL – Zandri Burger

# THE WEEPING PRINCE

# And The Mansion in Sand

# ALICE VL

# ZANDRI BURGER

# The Weeping Prince & The Mansion in Sand

At the tender age of 17, Scarlett Rose was the well-known, well-liked and respectable daughter of the only preacher in Carmel, Pastor Joseph and his wife, Lily Horak.

Until then, Scarlett Rose had presented herself with utmost dignity and led her life as a teenager in a proper and orderly fashion, as was expected from her.

She by no means at all questioned her father's strict and commanding rules, while she remained blithe and content to oblige under his authority.

From the moment she met Blade Bannister, it all changed. All she had ever thought was true and correct had altered instantly. She rebelled against her father and her Church. She fearlessly questioned him and his religion.

Blade Bannister transported her into a world of excitement, exhilaration and love, while she was keen to surrender entirely to his power over her.

For the first time in her life, she had fallen unreservedly and unconditionally in love with the boy from the wrong side of the tracks whose broken and shattered family had been at war with the Horak's for centuries before.

Scarlett remained unerringly devoted to her love for him while exploring the stars and her make-believe enchantment through her sand castles.

She in no way at all could foresee or predict the devastation the future would hold when she discovered Pastor Joe's horrifying and mortal betrayal.

The world Blade had sworn to rescue her to, no longer existed as the crushing and devastating revelation made way for an entirely shattering, yet unexpected forever.

# CONTENTS

The Weeping Prince & The Mansion in Sand

٢

# PASTOR JOSEPH'S DAUGHTER

"Scarlett Rose! Scar! Wait for me!"

Scarlett Rose Horak turned around abruptly when she heard her name being frantically and urgently called out from behind her.

"Hey Alethea, what's up?"

When Alethea reached her, she promptly bent over in a desperate attempt to inhale a mouthful of air.

"Let me just catch my breath! You always make me run after you!"

Scarlett giggled sympathetically as she watched her friend respire profoundly. She anxiously attempted to take in bottomless breaths of fresh air in rapid succession of one another.

"Maybe you should learn to keep up."

Scarlett chuckled once more before Alethea glared at her with downright disgust which was at once, surprisingly evident on her face.

"Maybe, you shouldn't always be in such a hurry to get home!"

Alethea yelled impatiently as she stood up right before placing her hands on her hips while noticeable irritation was unmistakable in her eyes.

Scarlett Rose had first met Alethea in primary school shortly after the Scott family had transferred to Carmel from Sydney, Australia almost seven years ago.

She had laid eyes on the unruly and enormously overenthusiastic Alethea when the Scotts had attended her father's Church for the very first time one Sunday morning just as Alethea was about to begin school at Carmel Elementary.

Alethea and Scarlett had instantaneously become solid friends, even though their divergences were remarkably astonishing; one that Pastor Joe often described as an improbable alliance.

Scarlett Rose was raised in an unreservedly regimented, stringent upbringing while Alethea's parents permitted their daughter a fair amount of independence. They had barely any aspiration to impose harsher rules in their household; the Scotts believed that it was vital for Alethea to wander without restraint and on her own requisites.

As would be expected, it incensed Pastor Joe to witness her often boisterous behavior and he recurrently questioned her disruptive vocabulary which had left him with absolute disgust and more often than not, entirely flabbergasted.

Alethea Scott was an only child to her parents, Mary and Michael Scott. Mary delighted in her role as a stay-at-home mom whose entire universe centered around her daughter, while Michael earned a respectable living as a popular banker who found the segregation and reclusion in Carmel enormously tantalizing.

Alethea was tremendously spoilt, yet she was beautiful and exceptionally popular in school amongst her peers and her teachers. Even though she was enormously strident and gregarious, there was a definite virtuousness and loveliness about her.

Her long legs were responsible for her brilliant athletic achievements and which secured her a copious amount of soccer trophies, while Scarlett on the other hand was enclosed in a petite frame that showed no ambition for any type of sports. Scarlett's academic accomplishments far outweighed any other student in Carmel, and she would contentedly stay behind after school in an attempt to assist Alethea with her homework, who demonstrated little to no interest in achieving academically.

They were a dubious pair; Alethea's fair hair was kept short and manageable while her hazel eyes and utterly pale complexion were flawlessly balanced. Scarlett on the other hand, kept her dark tresses long which emphasized her arctic blue eyes and olive complexion. Alethea was thunderous and excitable while Scarlett was agonizingly inhibited and particularly self-conscious and soft spoken.

As Alethea's parents allowed and encouraged their daughter to discover her passage in the course of her life on her own stipulations, Scarlett's parents possessed an often-irrational predisposition to shield her from the world; from external unconstructive influence and less than favorable, yet impending decisions.

Alethea was permitted to be present at any and all societal gatherings that would encourage her acceptance into the social order, while Scarlett was kept veiled behind the high walls and locked gates of their home. Alethea had by the age of eighteen, dated numerous of boys while Scarlett was sternly prohibited from any contact with the contrary gender.

The Weeping Prince & The Mansion in Sand

Scarlet Rose Horak's father was affectionately honored by the citizens of Carmel as Pastor Joe, leaving Scarlett under immense pressure to advocate and preserve a regimented and God-fearing facade.

Unlike Alethea, Scarlett Rose was born in Carmel seventeen years before to Pastor Joseph and Lily Horak who had assertively established heredity in the quaint little village with a population of barely ten thousand inhabitants. As with Scarlett and her older brother Matthew, both Pastor Joseph and Lily Horak were born in Carmel where until recently, Pastor Joe's parents owned vast farming lands dating back to hundreds of years earlier.

The Horak family came from an extensive line of Old Order Amish who were a family of traditionalist Christian church fellowships with Swiss Anabaptist origins. They were closely related to, but entirely distinct from Mennonite churches. The Horaks, to this day are known for simple living, plain dress, and utter unwillingness to adopt the many conveniences of modern technology.

When Matthew and Scarlett were born, Pastor Joe was adamant that they refrain from formal education, but Lily insisted that their children attend school in Carmel just as any other child would. It often caused severe tension between Pastor Joe and Lily, yet he hesitantly surrendered to her only demand and reluctantly agreed.

When the Horak family sold their lands to property developers who were in the process of establishing Carmel, they had volunteered to remain in the village and were warmheartedly identified for their arrangement and contribution of breathing life into a pristine new town. As the years passed by, Carmel had expanded into a bustling village that was essentially funded by fishermen and local business owners.

Carmel was entirely self-supportive and although most farm lands were lost to the erection of the village, the city continued to cultivate a small amount of land that surrounded Carmel. There were sufficient areas of land that were devoted to agricultural processes with the primary objective of producing food and other crops; the basic facility in food production.

Specific areas were used for specialised units such as vegetable farms, fruit farms, dairy, pig and poultry farms, including land that was used for the production of natural fibres, biofuel and other commodities.

Carmel was a strikingly beautiful parish that had effortlessly attracted visitors from all ends of the world. The impression created with a number of holiday makers were that the residents of Carmel were disinclined and entirely unenthusiastic to evolve and advance forward with the ever-changing times. The era of modernization had remained on the back-burner for as long as was possible; for as long as Pastor Joe deemed it essential. Other than only a handful of households, technology had not quite found its way into the homes of the Carmel residents.

The village boasted with immaculate and beautiful white beaches, while at the same time, the endless Rocky Mountains were a luminous vision that almost engulfed the entire village.

Carmel summers were moderately warm while their winters fell into sub-zeroing temperatures and were bitter cold. The first flakes of snow had habitually begun to fall each year in the first week of December while the last of the snow would barely begin to subside as January was about to come to an end. Tourists adored and highly thought of their beautiful village and it seemed at times that Pastor Joseph Horak was the self-proclaimed Mayor of Carmel.

Pastor Joseph Horak was the cranium of the only Cathedral in Carmel and he would effortlessly lead a congregation in excess of a hundred members on any regular

Sunday. He had erected his Church in the dead-centre of the village, and he took enormous pride in the fact that it had become the largest seated house of worship in the world, yet in the most minuscule little town on the face of the earth.

Pastor Joe was exclusively devoted and utterly committed to his faith as he unerringly conducted sermons for up to four days a week, yet on Sundays, morning and evening services were compulsory. Other than preaching sermons from the altar, he had established a youth centre for troubled teens or simply teens that were deficient of discipline and authority.

Pastor Joe was an enormous enthusiast of obedience and restraint, and he delighted in the participation of instilling worth and unquestionable morals in children from an immensely young age. When Scarlett turned sixteen, she was deep-rooted into the faith by Pastor Joe and was at once assigned the obligation and title of Sunday School Teacher to the younger children. Lily had been the Choir Master for several years, while both mother and daughter were devoted choir members of the Horak Christian Fellowship.

Pastor Joe disqualified music and social get-togethers at both the high and primary schools while he implored local pubs and restaurants to entirely abandon any and all events that included rock and roll or dancing of any sort. He was wholly persuaded that rock and roll in particular, resulted in a powerful, yet rebellious impact on society. He was certain that it entirely influenced daily life, fashion, attitudes and language in a way few other social developments have equalled.

He particularly associated rock and roll music with sex and drugs, and he regularly reminded the citizens of Carmel that rock and roll stars were known as hard-drinking, hard-living characters. Pastor Joe had significant restrictions and limitless rules, one of which were fashion. He would strictly impress upon the towns folk that clothing reflects norms about standards of modesty, religion, gender, and social status. It was absolutely imperative to Pastor Joe that all women were appropriately covered and wore relatively loose fitting trousers. Perfume and cosmetics were banned for all girls under the age of twenty-one, while married woman and mothers were compelled to become successful and devoted home-makers.

On the unusual occasion that a divorce had taken place between a husband and a wife, Pastor Joe would permit a single mother to take up suitable employment, primarily to support her household. Pastor Joe would barely approve of divorce and would in more cases than one, prohibit a divorce from being realized.

He would persistently sermonize that marriage was intended to be a permanent, covenantal relationship between a man, who was to protect and provide for his wife, and a woman, who was to remain monogamous to her husband. It was only in the direst of circumstances that he would surrender his blessing. Pastor Joe had created a lifestyle that delivered his sermons under an immensely harsh and uncompromising code, as he dynamically surmized that his morality and etiquette was merely to preserve the integrity of the community.

Scarlett Rose was elected as Prominent Leader of her final year at Carmel High School, precisely as her brother had been appointed barely two years before her. Even though Scarlett was wholly reluctant to embrace the role as an overseer to the senior classes of Carmel High, she was compelled to accept the task at hand in a desperate attempt to please her father.

She was under prodigious strain to guide and promote by example, though she felt at times she would buckle miserably under the severe pressure. She was enormously captivated by the freedom that was bestowed upon her peers and she often coveted the girls that were entitled to lavish abundantly, often recklessly in birthday parties and social gatherings. Scarlett and Matthew's birthday celebrations usually meant a quiet dinner, specially prepared for them by their mother.

To honor their births, she would happily bake a birthday cake and they would come together as a family of four and enjoy the feast prepared by Lily. In no way at all, did Pastor Joe permit a party of any sort and he would refuse a visit or gifts from any of their friends at school. Lily normally crocheted or knitted each a sweater, but under no circumstances were gifts allowed for birthdays or Christmas.

August in Carmel usually signified the end of summer, yet it also meant that there were merely three months left of the school year. As was the case each year, the Student Committee would submit a written request to Pastor Joe for permission to host a formal dance just as winter was about to begin, and as per all the years before, he sternly and abruptly declined their request without so much as a justification or explanation.

It would anger him immensely that the students of Carmel possessed the audacity to appeal for such an outrageous request of him. He would regularly question the parenting skills of the other parents and he would at all times, unwaveringly reassure himself of the fact that he was acting in the very best interests of the community.

Pastor Joe possessed a mean streak; he in no way permitted another to partake in a two-way, opposing conversation with him. He would abruptly interrupt any discussion that he would deem unsuitable and focus the attention back to himself, showing little to no interest in anyone else.

Should a dialogue fail to result in agreement with his own views, he would deliberately and abruptly correct, dismiss or ignore the relevance of the discussion. Although he would come across as exceedingly charismatic and persuasive, he undoubtedly possessed an exaggerated sense of self-importance while he was convinced that others could in no way survive without his magnificent contribution.

Scarlett was utterly repulsed by Pastor Joe's unequivocal stubborness and his unwavering determination to cage and imprison the youth of Carmel. He was admittedly convinced that evil lurked in each record or song, while satan lingered patiently, ready to pounce with each social gathering. More than anything else, Pastor Joe absolutely detested and denied same-sex relationships; he made no secret of the fact that he condemned homosexual acts as sinful while fervently maintaining that homosexual sex was forbidden in the Bible.

He would without any hesitation, bar any practising gay man or woman from his Church and he would condemn their souls into an eternity in hell. Pastor Joe became increasingly demanding of his wife Lily as the years had passed by. He would often remind her of the fact that his expectations were not entirely due to the reality that she was the pastor's wife, but primarily as a result of her acting as a good Christian wife. It was imperative that she submit to the Lord and to him; that she should please her husband and educate the younger women in their village. Rather than resent the differences between her and an ordinary Christian woman, Lily willingly embraced her role and accepted her stance as a gift from God.

Pastor Joe was overwhelmingly burdened to impose discipline and gesticulation in his children. Other than Scarlett being the only daughter and youngest child, her brother Matthew was barely two years older than her. Pastor Joe and Lily were refined and distinguished members and popular leaders of their community.

It was of the utmost importance that their children appear proper and of an impressive class. From an enormously young age, Matthew and Scarlett were to address their parents as 'Sir' or 'Ma'am', especially in the company of outsiders, and disobeying his authority and subsequent set of rules were in no way a deliberation that had ever crossed his children's minds. Pastor Joe in no way at all viewed his children as comparable to any other child in his congregation.

His mind convinced him that they were spiritual superstars solely due to the fact that they were his offspring; the pastor's children. He was adamant that their identities were based on his vocation and that it was essential for stricter regulations and the subsequent enforcement of unyielding limitations.

Lily on the other hand, appeared extraordinarily reserved from a world detached from Pastor Joe and his Church. Scarlett often referred to her as the long-suffering wife of the only pastor in town while she felt immense pity for her mother. Lily would frequently console Scarlett when her father was not nearby to witness Scarlett's utter wretchedness.

At times, Lily had intentionally undermined Pastor Joe's wishes which would result in a Sunday morning sermon that would brutally show aggression towards her behavior, unbeknownst to the fellow members of his congregation that his entire sermon was intended as a warning for his wife and children.

Years before, Lily had reluctantly admitted to the reality that she was keen to dissociate from him, but the laws of his Church ensured that it was virtually unattainable. She unenthusiastically and half-heartedly persisted under the statute of Pastor Joe but would once in a while; engage in a hopeless endeavor to shelter Scarlett and Matthew from his blinding wrath.

His subsequent tantrums and overreaction was the source of countless of arguments in the Horak home and although he would blindly shatter a dinner plate or a coffee mug against a wall; he by no means lifted his hands to his wife or children in antagonism. During moments of Pastor Joe's extreme rage, Scarlett would escape into a world that would sweep her into an imaginary life inside of her sand castle.

She would effortlessly shut off from the fighting and shouting and she would run away into a world that welcomed her with open arms where rules and regulations no longer existed. Scarlett longed for a life without Pastor Joe and all the restraints that was passed onto her as the pastor's daughter. She yearned for love and acceptance and she craved the sovereignty that she was certain she would someday find.

Pastor Joe was fraught to prohibit his children from attaching themselves to informal friendships. He would habitually insist that Lily accompany Scarlett whenever it was compulsory for her to venture out to the city mall, or perhaps, attend an after school gathering or concert.

He banned her entirely from sleepovers, yet he once in a while permitted a stopover to Alethea while on condition that he drops her off and picks her up after a short visit. Pastor Joe had paltry to barely any tolerance of Alethea's deportment. He would repeatedly mention to Lily that she entirely lacked obedience and that her conduct was awful and wholly inappropriate.

Even though he found Scarlett's friendship with Alethea appalling, he submitted to the fact that they were devoted members of his congregation and it was significant that Scarlett maintain a scanty number of friends. Pastor Joe's opinion on Scarlett's dress code had barely wavered since she was a little girl. He regularly informed her of the fact that men were entirely visual, and he was adamant that his daughter dress appropriately and modestly.

Her hair was to be tied back neatly while her dresses were long and shapeless. On the odd occasion that he would allow her to dress in jeans, he was adamant that they were loose fitting.

Matthew on the other hand, was spared the entirety of his father's outbursts once he had left the so-called sanctuary of his childhood home to attend university barely 300 miles away in a town called Vilars. Matthew was keen to study engineering and was thrilled when the news arrived that he was accepted into the University of Vilars without hesitation or restriction.

Pastor Joe and Matthew often came to severe blows due to Matthew's preference of career, while he was obstinate that his son follow in his foot steps and become the next pastor of Carmel. Matthew wholly refused to entertain the notion and devoid of Pastor Joe's blessing or approval, he applied to universities of his selection in the field of his choosing. When Pastor Joe threatened to interrupt the funding for his enrolment, Lily was certain that they were about to engage in a violent stand-off. Pastor Joe reluctantly surrendered when he realized that Matthew was unswerving in his decision. Matthew was a tall, sturdy young man that would appeal to many young women in Carmel who would regularly throw themselves at his feet.

Scarlett would habitually taunt Matthew about his appeal while he would become bashful almost with each one of her ridicules. Scarlett would often smile while gazing admiringly at her brother; she was entirely attentive to his ignorism of his masculine beauty. His dark hair and arctic blue eyes confirmed his genetic association to Scarlett, yet their personalities differed altogether.

Scarlett was glaringly reserved and visibly obedient, while Matthew was far more sociable and who had developed willpower of his own. He would regularly urge Scarlett to take a stand in opposition to her father, but Scarlett would concede to the authenticity that the conflict between them would be devastatingly fear-provoking for their mother. On one such a confrontation between Matthew and his father, and only moments after Pastor Joe had stormed out of their home, Matthew turned to his mother,

"Why don't you just leave the man?" Matthew would yell out in anger and utter frustration.

Lily would lower her head while unreservedly disgraced and dissatisfied by the woman she had become. "Its God's will, Matty."

Matthew would storm out of the house and make his way onto the beach where he would linger until he had calmed down. Scarlett would often find him staring out over the ocean; she would sit beside him in silence while holding his hand into hers in a desperate attempt to comfort him.

"I can't wait to leave here, Scar." He would disclose sorrowfully, yet in unreserved resentment and frustration.

"Don't leave me here without you, Matty."

She would plead for him to take her with him. They would converse late into the night while Matthew would anxiously beg her to see her final year of school through before she too, could join him in Vilars. Scarlett was deathly frightened of her father, but at the same time, she was terrified of leaving her mother behind at the mercy of Pastor Joe.

"Scar, please come sleep over tonight! Jackson is taking me to the opening of The Doll's House and you know my brother, he will probably bugger off with his friends and leave me all alone there."

"I can't Ally, you know Pastor Joe would never allow it? Besides, I have to go to Church."

"Church? On a Friday night?"

"Yeah. He's called for an emergency choir rehearsal."

Ally frowned dejectedly while she felt enormous compassion for Scarlett at once.

"Come on, Scar! You're already in Church six days a week...why would he call for a choir rehearsal on a Friday night?"

Scarlett lowered her head as she realized that outside of

school and Church, she had no life at all.

"Pastor Joe won't allow it, Ally."

Alethea placed her arms around her friend, "Just ask him, just try, okay?"

Scarlett Rose bowed her head in despondence as she convinced herself entirely that to so much as solicit Pastor Joe's consent would result in a fierce and hostile response from him.

"Ally, your parents are different, while my father, well, he's Pastor Joe."

"Do you think he would let us have a prom this year?"

"Come on, Ally. You know he would never allow it. He has to protect the young ones from the devil's clutches."

Scarlett and Alethea simultaneously erupted into laughter.

"Yeah, yeah … whatever."

Alethea was at once repelled by Pastor Joe's ignorance.

"You don't have to be so perfect, Scarlett."

"Yes, I do …"

Scarlett waved goodbye to Alethea while she hurriedly made her way down the path that led out onto the beach. It was a path she would take often and where she would spend an hour on the beach of sheer bliss and unreserved tranquility, while fiercely endeavoring to build her sand castles unaided and in silence.

Day after day and for most of her life, Scarlett would lose herself while erecting her mansions of sand, only to devastatingly discover that the tide had washed them out as the next sunrise had broken. She would grow increasingly pessimistic and discouraged to learn that she was powerless to construct a castle sturdy enough to withstand each forceful and ruthless tide.

As a little girl, she dreamed of reaching her mansions in the morning to discover that they were standing as tall and as proud as she had left them the night before and she fantasized about finding her mansions, blindingly lit up by the stars of the night.

Yet, each morning, they were washed away by the waves of the preceding night, and she would habitually gather her sand and relentlessly begin again.

She was convinced that someday, her sand castles would endure the profound winds and the forceful tides of the ocean.

Alice VL – Zandri Burger

The Weeping Prince & The Mansion in Sand

From an enormously young age, Scarlett was enthralled by the Legend of the Weeping Prince when her mother once told her the story of how Mizolitlo, an artist lived out the rest of his days building the foremost and finest sand castles the world has ever seen.

Just as with the Weeping Prince, Scarlett was convinced that her dreams were waiting for her in her sand castle; an alternate reality that she could switch to whenever this one had become too overwhelming for her.

Although the Weeping Prince perished at the hands of the first Spanish explorers in the early part of the 16th century, many still proudly speak his name with enormous admiration. To this day, some have claimed to have mysteriously found immense structures of sand that were constructed overnight near the water's shore.

There were others that claimed they could hear faint cries during the brightest of moons and tranquil of nights. Scarlett Rose adored her mother's narration of Mizolitlo and as a child; she would incessantly plead with Lily to tell her the story of the Weeping Prince one more time.

Scarlett was convinced that they were paranormal mansions of enchantment; she was certain that somewhere in her sand castles, mysterious fascination was waiting to find her. Perhaps, her own prince would appear to her and carry her away to a world of enthrallment and unrestricted freedom.

Scarlett was convinced that there was someone out there for her that would show up and seize her into his arms while he swept her away; away from Carmel and away from Pastor Joe. She dreamed of the man that would fiercely protect her; who was by no means at all demoralized by her father. Scarlett longed for her prince that would sweep her away from a life she was bitterly discontented in.

Scarlett hurriedly placed her satchel down beside her, and without delay, she began to gather sand while she reflected back on the Weeping Prince as she would do each time she prepared to build her sand castle. She would mold and form each corner post with painstaking accuracy, and when one seemed a little off beam, she would break the sand castle down, and begin again.

What the Weeping Prince could never succeed in, was to light up his castles by the light of the moon and the stars. Scarlett dreamed of building the world's finest sand castle that humanity had ever seen and that would light up even the darkest of nights. She would become the Weeping Prince's princess and together they would leap into her sand castle and escape into a world of unrestricted fascination.

Scarlett was convinced that her very own fairy tale was caught up in the halls and the walls of her sand castles that were being washed away by the tide almost as though on schedule. Each day, she was certain that she was losing one more day in her voyage of her brand-new tomorrows, but Scarlett knew that until then, she had to remain Pastor Joe's faultless daughter.

When she glanced at her wristwatch, Scarlett realized that she had spent a significant amount of time longer on her sand castle than she had normally set aside for.

"I must go now, sand dreams. Please stand strong. I know that between the stars and the ocean somewhere, there is magic that will someday, light you up. I believe in you...and I believe in magic."

She smiled dreamily before she grabbed her satchel and hurried home along the beach.

When Scarlett reached their colonial house only meters away from the beach, she stumbled upon her mother who was frantic to find her.

"Scarlett Rose!" Lily bellowed as Scarlett walked through

the front door.

"Sorry Ma'am. I was at the beach and…I was sidetracked by the sand castles."

"You and those sand castles! You know how your father feels about you running off to build your sand castles!"

"I know mama, but he never lets me go anywhere? I'm not doing anything wrong."

Lily lowered her head as she harshly continued spreading sandwiches for a quick lunch before choir practice.

"You are not to disobey your father, Scar. He loves you and he knows best. God has given him a great deal of responsibility and it isn't easy for him. We must stand by him and try to lighten his load."

Scarlett sighed dreadfully as she listened to her mother reprimand her, "I know, mama. Where is Pastor Joe?"

Scarlett was at once aware of his absence. "Out at the barn. He should be back any minute or else we'll be late for choir practice."

"Mama…Ma'am, Ally asked me to spend the night at her place. Please can I go?"

Scarlett was agonizingly conscious of what her mother's response would be, yet she engaged in a courageous effort to alter her mother's response.

Lily placed the butter knife on the counter at once, and turned to face Scarlett while sheer fury was evident on her mother's face, "Why? You know no good can come of spending the night at the Scott's. No Scar, your father will have none of it."

Lily picked up the knife and began to slice through the sandwiches.

"You never let me go anywhere! I'm not even allowed to make friends. What does Pastor Joe think I'm going to do?"

Scarlett raised her voice while frustration had begun to overwhelm her entire body.

"What did you say, Scarlett? Is that any way to speak to your mother?"

She was at once startled to find her father appear from behind her.

"Nothing Sir."

"Nothing? Did I hear correctly when you asked your mother if you could spend the night at the Scotts?"

Scarlett lowered her head as her tears began to shimmer in her eyes. She could barely face him, let alone respond to his sudden outburst.

"Satan is all around us, Scarlett! You are duty-bound to wrestle through all the mortal pleasures. It is either that you are for the world, or you are for God. Which is it, Scar?"

Her father had become enraged at once. "Look at me, Scarlett Rose!"

She lifted her eyes and gazed intently at Pastor Joe.

"Which is it?"

"I am a child of the King, father." She whispered hoarsely as her body had begun to shudder.

"You will have a sandwich and afterwards, you go get ready for choir practice."

"I was just asking, Pastor Joe."

"You are not to ask again, is that clear Scarlett?"

"Yes, sir."

Scarlett hastily ran upstairs, anxious to reach a secure remoteness from her father, unwilling to permit her father from witnessing her agonizing tears. She collapsed onto her bed while her tears had enthusiastically begun to roll from her eyes.

She was wholeheartedly susceptible to the reality that there had to be more to life other than being held incarcerated almost as a redundant and caged animal. For as long as Scarlett could recall, they were altogether shielded from the outside world and the sinister souls, as Pastor Joe would habitually remind them of, that encircled them.

Those were the shadowy souls that eternally lingered in anticipation of a grasp, just as a snake would slither out of sight and strike his prey when it was at its most vulnerable; murky souls that would lurk amongst the youth and wait patiently for their defenselessness before they were to strike.

In no way at all, did Pastor Joe permit a television set or a mobile phone in their home. The landline was kept securely locked at all times and was merely used for crisis calls or for when it was imperative to reach Pastor Joe as he was mandated to perform last rites.

Scarlett would often catch her mother listening to the radio in clandestine, and more often than not, she immensely pitied her mother's confinement, just as her own internment by Pastor Joe.

Scarlett would often solicit permission from him to revise her school work at the local library where study literature was freely available for certain tasks and projects. Unlike her class mates, Scarlett had no access to the internet which left the library as her only source of information.

As she would stroll through the streets of Carmel en route to the library, she would be persistently attentive to Pastor Joe surreptitiously following her. Scarlett glared straight ahead of her and barely greeted any person walking by out of fear that he would accuse her of socializing outside of his Church.

As she would leave the library, she would once again catch a glimpse of him as he sat in his car while fiercely attempting to catch her out in an untruth. It was exhausting for Scarlett Rose; as desperate as she had become to please him and as valiantly as she would commit to obeying him, it seemed to her as though his faith in her had been distorted for no reason at all.

She was dismayed and utterly contaminated by his typical accusations while she unwaveringly attempted to restore the faith he had shown her when she was barely a little girl.

As the choral group took their seats in the first four rows of his Church, Pastor Joe abruptly made his way up to the altar.

Scarlett lowered her Melodica and gazed incredulously up at her father.

"Beloved brothers and sisters, it has come to my attention that there are members of this very congregation that have requested in writing, a year-end dance for the high school seniors? I believe the word is prom?"

Pastor Joe gazed in fury as the members of his choir bowed their heads in devastating dishonor.

"There shall be no moving of bodies to the tunes of rock and roll music. As long as I am Pastor of the community, there will be no worshipping of irresponsible partying amongst any of the congregation and especially not the youth. An ordinance is in place that prohibits all and any contact between men and women in such a sexually suggestive manner. Are we clear?"

Pastor Joe had raised his voice as his annoyance had escalated. "We are not animals! We are not beasts! We co-exist in a proper and orderly fashion. Before long, you will be requesting the legalization of marijuana and alcohol. What will be next? Drugs? Let us bow our heads and beg for repentance."

Scarlett was at once mortified by her father's sudden insolence and when she hurriedly glanced around her, she discovered that the entire choral group had closed their eyes in unison and fervently begged for exculpation.

She was frantic to discover whom it was precisely that the population of Carmel had worshipped; was it God or was it in actual fact, Pastor Joe?

His unrelenting pursuit of gratification from vanity and egotistic admiration was unmistakable. His inflated sense of self-entitlement had been whispered about by all members at one point in time, but none possessed the courage to take a stand in opposition to Pastor Joe.

Scarlett often bore witness to his social influence that persistently aimed to alter the behavior or perception of his flock through abusive, deceptive, and underhanded tactics. He was a great manipulator while his delusion usually came at another's expense, costing them dearly.

The Horak family arrived home barely an hour after choir practice before Pastor Joe hurriedly retreated into his study, while Lily dashed into the kitchen. "Scarlett!" Her mother anxiously called out to her.

"Yes, Ma'am?"

"Please lay the dining room table. Dinner should be

warm in a few minutes."

"All right, mama."

Once Pastor Joe was seated at the head of the table, Lily and Scarlett took their seats at the oversized dining room table. Pastor Joe took each by the hand while he calmly and unhurriedly said grace. They sat in silence for only a moment before Pastor Joe abruptly turned to Scarlett,

"Scarlett Rose, whose idea was this whole prom and dance spectacle?"

He glared exasperatingly at her while Scarlett realized that his irritation had in no way subsided. Scarlett lowered her head for an instant, before she glanced back at him.

"I don't know, father?"

She was abundantly perceptive to the reality that Alethea had drawn up the questionable petition which was signed by all the senior students, including Scarlett, and handed to Mr. Myers, Principal of Carmel High School. They had eagerly posed the question one Monday morning in the school hall while Mr. Myers and the school teachers were present.

Mr. Myers agreed at once to the proposition of a prom,

with an uncontested stipulation that Pastor Joseph Horak bestows his blessing upon the school and upon the students.

"Well, I'll have none of it. It's toxic and utterly inappropriate." He snapped irately at the mere thought of merry-making by a bunch of teenagers.

"I mean, dad ... sir, its just dancing and one final get-together for all the seniors. Is that so bad?" Scarlett thrust herself into a courageous effort of challenging her irate father.

Pastor Joe harshly dropped his knife and fork onto his plate before he furiously turned back to Scarlett. "It's not just dancing. It's the work of the devil, of satan. I will not permit you, or any other teenager in this town to disrespect or rebel against God. Is that clear? This is how it all starts, Scarlett. This is how satan invades us...is that what you want?"

Scarlett lowered her head once again. "No, sir."

Lily at once felt pity for Scarlett and the remainder of the seniors of Carmel High. She acknowledged the fact that they were youthful, and she was keen for the youngsters of Carmel to engage in at least one social gathering before the year was finally over.

She was unexpectedly distraught by the realization that

Scarlett's flame was dying inside of her, and it scared her to consider the fact that someday soon, she would depart just as Matthew had absconded at the very instant he was able to. Lily was desperate for Scarlett to travel and discover the world while absorbing all there was for her to gain knowledge of.

She could barely recall her daughter's smile, let alone her laughter and was devastated by the actuality that they had sheltered her so exclusively.

"Joseph, I don't think a prom would be the worst idea. You and I could volunteer to chaperone? I think it's exactly what the youth need." Lily veiled her fear as she matter-of-factly brought forward a proposal that might find with the Pastor's approval.

Pastor Joe had become infuriated at once and when Scarlett glanced at him, she was aware that his eyes had become blood shot. He slammed his fists onto the dining room table in utter fury while Scarlett and Lily were at once startled by the enormous thump.

The entire table had shuddered for an instant, before Lily took her serviette from her lap and dabbed at her lips.

"My wife questioning me?"

The Weeping Prince & The Mansion in Sand

The Pastor's wife had found herself in conflict with her husband for the first time since they were married almost twenty-five years ago. "Should I call you when I find your badly beaten and brutally raped daughter's body in a gutter somewhere here in Carmel. Is it you who will explain that you allowed her to roam the streets of the village at night which made her vulnerable to prowlers. Will you identify your only daughter's body in a ditch after a drug-fuelled, booze filled night out on the town dancing?"

He grabbed at Lily's wrist as she turned to face Pastor Joe, "We are going to lose her, Joseph. You cannot imprison her in this way!"

"Pastor Joe! Let go of mom's arm!"

Scarlett shouted out to her father as she ferociously attempted to release her mother's arm from his grip. Pastor Joe retreated at once before he turned to Scarlett, "You are ungrateful, Scarlett Rose. The dark prince is holding you firmly in your clutches. We must pray, at once!"

He took her hand before she hurriedly pulled away from him.

"Don't pray for my soul, Pastor Joe. Pray for your own.

You are smothering me. You and your rules!"

Pastor Joe brought out the Scripture at once and spent the most part of an hour thrashing through paragraphs and subsections of imminent sin and suitable punishment. He begged Scarlett to repent and seek absolution for her immoral thoughts and when they bowed their heads in prayer; he pleaded with God to exonerate her from the worldly temptations.

While Scarlett had begun clearing the dining room table, Lily made her way into the kitchen and hurriedly began washing up. Scarlett handed her their dinner plates before she turned to face her mother,

"Thank you, Ma'am…thank you for standing up for me." She placed her arms around her mother's neck and held her firmly against her.

"It was of no good, Scar. He will never change."

"I know mama, but thank you anyway."

Scarlett climbed into bed shortly before nine o'clock. Her mind at once drifted back to Alethea. For a moment, she envied her friend's independence and free-will while she wondered whether she would in fact; attend the opening of The Doll's House. Scarlett glanced at her wristwatch and instantaneously leaped from her bed.

Without a sound, she slid on a pair of jeans and a sweater, before she quietly locked her bedroom door. Scarlett sat down at the end of her bed while she contemplated her next move. She was desperately in need of a night out; away from Pastor Joe and away from the four smothering walls of her bedroom.

She was convinced that if he had caught her out, she would pay dearly for her sins for many years to come but her eagerness to be amongst her friends was overwhelming her.

Scarlett opened her bedroom window only slightly, but adequate to climb through before she hurriedly made her way down the lattice against their home. Once she safely reached the ground, she developed into a rapid sprint, and breathlessly ran the two blocks to Alethea's house.

When she reached her friend's home, she hurriedly made her way around to the rear of the house and tossed tiny pebbles directly at her window in a frantic attempt to alert Alethea of her presence. When Alethea spotted her, she hurriedly made her way downstairs and out the back door, where she found Scarlett waiting for her. "Scar?"

Alethea was at once baffled and anxious by her presence, while she was abundantly perceptive to Pastor Joe's boundaries and insufferable rules.

"I know, I know. I snuck out the house."

"You did what?"

"I snuck out, Alethea. They won't let me go anywhere! I'm so tired of Father Joe's unreasonable expectations."

Scarlett became unreservedly crestfallen at once, "I really wanted to go to The Doll's House with you."

She whispered apprehensively.

"Then we'll go, Scar. Give me two ticks and I'll be back. Its four blocks from here, we'll make it in no time. You know your father's going to slaughter you, right?"

"Only if he finds out."

# BLADE BANNISTER

As they strolled timidly into The Doll's House, Scarlett was at once aware of an unbefitting emotion while she was glaringly conscious of the fact that she was an absolute foreigner to the night life in Carmel.

She had never before witnessed the get-together of a crowd whose sole purpose was to consume alcohol and dance to the music that was bellowing from all around the club. The lights were dimmed while the stench of cigarette smoke and alcohol filled the air.

Scarlett glanced around her and noticed at once that clubbers, as Alethea referred to, were smiling a little too enthusiastically while nodding at whatever discussions they were enthralled in. The dance hall was disorienting large, while the ceilings were extremely high. Although, some people were clearly together, Scarlett found very few couples dancing in pairs.

It seemed terribly bizarre to her that the younger of the clubbers were dancing on their own as they stood motionlessly, yet violently shaking their heads. Scarlett giggled at the odd behavior but at the same time, she was utterly astounded to find regular Church goers indulging in the night life.

She had in no way before experienced such absolute, yet wonderful chaos, as she did when she intriguingly glanced around her.

"Oh, Pastor Joe would succumb to heart failure."

She thought silently as she brusquely followed Alethea to the pub and nervously ordered a glass of water. "Water, really?"

Alethea frowned before she instantly requested a beer for herself. Scarlett stared at her in amazement despite the fact that she admired her friend's gallantry. Scarlett glanced around once again and discovered that the club was filled to capacity as clubbers were squeezing past one another in an attempt to reach a table or to make their way onto the dance floor.

She glanced over to the jukebox and noticed what she considered to be a biker squad which entirely fascinated her. They were a group of four men who were seated at a table, entirely detached from the rest of the clubbers.

The youngest of the four continuously selected music on the jukebox and while her father condemned and banished any class of songs other than gospel, she thoroughly enjoyed the sudden rush that had surged through her as the music had come alive inside of her. She smiled often while entirely unaware that the youngest of the group had instantly noticed her.

From across the hall, Blade Bannister stood gazing at Scarlett who seemed entirely out of place between the countless clubbers and drinkers. He watched her often whilst he was keenly acquainted with the class of men that frequented night clubs.

"You keep an eye on that one, son." Long John Mackenzie nudged Blade as he stared at the young Scarlett who was sipping at her water. "She has no business here." Long John snapped as he turned back to his crew.

Blade Bannister was born into dire poverty roughly twenty-two years ago to Bobby and Kikki Bannister. Years before Blade's birth, the Bannister family proudly owned the majority of the farm lands that made up the town of Carmel as it were for years before his birth.

As with the Horak family, the Bannisters once lived in splendour and were highly regarded as one of the wealthiest families in the district. When the Bannister family was approached by Jethro-Horak Developments to sell their land, they steadfastly refused which resulted in tense relations between the Bannister and the Horak families.

Soon after the Horak family sold their lands solely for the development of Carmel, a devastating fire destroyed all crops and cattle on the Bannister lands. Unable to recuperate from their severe financial losses, the Bannisters were summarily evicted from their home shortly after the bank had foreclosed on their farm and surrounding lands. The Bannister men took up employment at the railways and were compelled to dwell in Carmel Railway's low-cost housing ever since.

Bobby Bannister toiled conscientiously to restore his family's reputation and dignity while desperate to support Kikki and their unborn child. When she passed away while giving birth to Blade, Bobby was entirely overwhelmed by the sudden and unexpected responsibilities of raising Blade as a single father. Shortly after Kikki's death, he wholly surrendered to liquor and shortly after Blade turned five years old; he was struck down by Gaucher disease and ruthlessly succumbed to the illness not quite three months later.

Blade was relentlessly tossed between a number of foster homes, yet since he was classified as an older boy that lacked the ability to bond with foster parents or siblings, he was in no way at all ever selected for adoption which resulted in the reality that he was moved around from home to home.

At the age of sixteen, he took off from his most recent foster home and returned to Carmel where Long John Mackenzie took him under his wing and taught him all there was to educate him on the repairing of motor cars and motorcycles. For the first time in Blade's entire existence and since Bobby had passed away, he had found acceptance and toleration with Long John and the rest of the Long John Motor Repair group; Rough Randy and Two Minute Tom.

Alethea had only just made her way onto the dance floor, when an older man approached Scarlett. She was overcome by a sudden bout of nausea as she became aware of the sickening aroma of perspiration, cigarettes and beer that were radiating from each pore of his body.

"Ey lil' lady." He slurred as he fixed his bloodshot, shimmering eyes on her. Scarlett became uncomfortable and unsettled at once.

"Hello." She was fraught to remain polite, yet nervous by the sudden and unwelcome interest in her.

"Can I get you a beer, lil' mama?"

"No thank you, sir."

Scarlett hurriedly turned away from him.

"Sir?"

He erupted into laughter while Scarlett lowered her head in utter mortification. Scarlett was at once horrified and terrified when he grabbed her by her arm in an attempt to regain her attention.

She had in no way at all ever been met by circumstances such as those of unsolicited awareness from an older, beer bellied stranger. She had no way of knowing precisely how to liberate herself from his clutches without causing a scene.

"Please let go of me."

She pleaded with the oversized bellied, alcohol stanching man who had no intention of retreating any time soon. He pulled her from her chair and pressed himself firmly against her, "Do you think you're better than me?"

Scarlett was terrified when she discovered how intimidating and unrelenting he had become while she was certain that her heart was ready to pound right out of her chest. Her hands had begun to tremble as he seized her into his arms while she was powerless to release herself from his ever-tightening grip.

She gazed at the bulky man in horror as her tears had

begun to glimmer while her fear was unmistakable in her eyes. Scarlett was desperate to remove herself from his clutches and as she stood pleading with him through her eyes, she was at once aware of an unexpected commotion that had begun to escalate around her.

She had barely had a moment to grasp all that was taking place around her when she felt a firm grasp tug on her arm. Before she was able to effusively identify with the chaos around her, she was hurriedly being led out through the crowd.

When she reached the outer surface of the club, Scarlett saw that the youngest man of the group from the jukebox that she had noticed earlier had frantically led our out of the club. "Quick! Put this on!"

He handed her a helmet before she placed it over her head in calamitous uncertainty.

"Climb up behind me!" He hollered out to her as she hurriedly hopped onto the motorcycle and sat nervously against him. She stared questioningly at him when she apprehensively noticed that he was carrying only a single helmet.

"Where's yours? Aren't you wearing one?"

"I'll be all right, hold on tight."

Scarlett held him firmly around his waist before he pulled away at an enormous and terrifying speed. When she turned to glance back, she noticed a group of sturdy men attempting to give chase. She tightened her grip around him and as she closed her eyes firmly, she anxiously buried her face in his neck.

They rushed through the streets of Carmel at what felt like a phenomenal speed to Scarlett while the wind blew wildly through her loose hanging tresses. He kept the motorcycle off the main roads of Carmel and the further they drove, the tighter she gripped him around his waist.

Scarlett had in no way before experienced a ride on a motorcycle before while she smiled rebelliously when she considered her father's utter horrification at the very notion.

She was at once aware of a feeling of exhilaration that had overwhelmed her while she felt liberation build up inside of her.

After they had been driving for a short while, the motorcycle came to an abrupt halt on a hilltop that overlooked the entire town. Scarlett hurriedly climbed off before she removed the helmet from her head.

"My father is going to kill me!" She became hysterical

almost at once while she considered her father's unquestionable wrath. He walked up to her and took the helmet from her before he placed it on the motorcycle. When he turned back to her, he let out a faint chuckle,

"Hi. I'm Blade Bannister."

"I'm … I'm Scarlett Rose Horak."

She was frenetic to remain courteous, while the terror had begun to overwhelm her.

"Oh God, seriously? You're Pastor Joe's daughter?"

Blade ran his hands through his hair while he contemplated the repercussions of racing around Carmel with Scarlett behind him on his motorcycle.

"Of all the girls tonight, it had to be you? The preacher man's only daughter? I am so screwed!"

Scarlett lowered her head as her entire body began to shudder.

"I snuck out of the house; he doesn't know. What if someone saw me?"

Once again, Scarlett became almost panic-stricken.

"Calm down, Scarlett. No-one saw you. I'll have you home in no time. Just calm down first."

He took her by her hand and led her to a rock where she sat down in silence. He sat down beside her and together, they gazed out over Carmel.

"I've never done this before, you know?"

She smiled despondently while desperate to explain that she was in no way of the wild and unruly sort.

"No shit."

He replied matter-of-factly while shaking his head. Scarlett giggled softly as she reflected on her one night of rebellion. She was keenly sensitive to a sense of freedom that had suddenly overwhelmed her and as she glanced guardedly over to Blade, she at once noticed his infallible appeal.

In Scarlett's caged mind, he was young, handsome and free. She was painfully alert to the fact that he was breathtakingly attractive while at the same time, she was certain that his eyes offered stories of a lifetime of misery. When she gazed into his eyes, she found herself carelessly plummeting into an emerald pool which she was convinced, she would hopelessly drown in. His striking appearance was at once veiled by his mesmerizing green eyes.

"So, you're still in school?"

"Yeah, my final year. You?"

"I work over at Long John Mackenzie's Garage with Rough Randy and Two Minute Tom. The guys that were with me at the club?"

He erupted into laughter as he witnessed Scarlett's absolute horror at their given names.

"That's not their real names, Scarlett, but to be honest, I have no inkling as to what their birth names are."

He chuckled as she began to grimace shamelessly.

"Oh. But, why would you agree to such horrid nick names?" She gazed blankly, but directly at Blade.

"Well, let's see. Long John Mackenzie is a really tall man; Rough Randy is crazy as hell and Two Minute Tom recalls nothing past two minutes."

Scarlett burst out laughing while Blade hurriedly justified the interpretation behind their names.

"That makes sense."

She giggled softly.

"Aren't you too young to work?"

"I'm twenty-two next month, you?"

"Seventeen, I'll be eighteen in the new year."

"So really? You've never been out before?"

Scarlett hesitated at once before she reluctantly responded in mortification, "No, never. Pastor Joe believes we can't live for the world and for God at the same time."

"Oh. So, what do you normally do with yourself? I mean, for fun?"

Blade at once felt immense compassion for her. Scarlett lowered her head while she considered all that her life consisted of.

"I go to school. I go to the beach and I go home. When I'm not at home, I am at Church."

She was unexpectedly ashamed of her enormously tedious existence.

"We go to Church a lot. You know, with my dad being Pastor and all?"

"So, what exactly motivated you to sneak out of your house?"

Scarlett gazed diffidently at him while he stared questioningly at her, "I just wanted to go out. Just once."

Blade stared at her as she spoke in a pliable, yet anxious and frightened manner. He had never before seen, let alone met a girl as beautiful, yet as untainted as Scarlett Rose Horak.

Her wintry blue eyes captivated him from the moment he gazed into them, but the wretchedness in her eyes told tales of a thousand disappointments.

He could sense that her trepidation had been rummaging inside of her for longer than she would care to disclose, and her tiny frame and petite build enticed unknown emotions of shielding while he was painfully responsive to a desperate need to safe guard her.

Blade was a loner who had no desire to seek human interaction.

He was enormously sensitive and painfully bashful while trauma and events from the past gave the impression of a social deviant. What was utterly challenging to comprehend, was the fact that Blade was in no way lonely, he was simply a loner.

"Well, I am glad you came out tonight, Scarlett. I am glad that we met."

He smiled diffidently at her before she turned to face him. She grinned shyly as she gazed into his eyes and when he smiled back at her, she turned away from him at once. "Me too."

They sat together in silence while they both wondered what it was that the other one was thinking. In a desperate effort to slice through the eerie silence, Blade told her about his passion for motorcycles and his equal enthusiasm for working on and repairing motor cars.

He mentioned how Long John Mackenzie reluctantly gave him the job when he was only seventeen years old after Blade categorically refused to complete high school or attend a suitable college.

He told Scarlett of his absolute lack of desire to obtain his high school diploma, yet he insisted he had achieved a world of experience while under Long John's thumb; more than he could ever learn from the benches at school.

"I am never going to have to know about history or biology, you know? My father worked with his hands, and so will I. Not all of us have to be doctors or lawyers; the world needs people like us. People that can get down and dirty, you know?"

"Yeah, but education is super important. Don't you want more for yourself? Don't you have dreams? I mean...don't you want to be someone some day?"

Scarlett was entirely mystified by his apparent lack of ambition. He gazed down at his hands while Scarlett stared questioningly at him.

"What is there? There's more to life than work and money. Besides, somebody has to repair cars. Like I said, we can't all be doctors and lawyers. That makes me someone, doesn't it?"

Scarlett stared at his hands when she abruptly realized that she was staring at hands that were in no way at all afraid of hard work. She smiled and nodded as she realized that she enormously admired his oil-stained and coarse hands.

Scarlett in turn, languorously told Blade about her love and admiration for sand castles and how desperate she was to build her mansion of sands by the exact method as the durability of stone.

She dreamily told him the tale of the Weeping Prince and how his sand castles are being discovered to this very day. She informed him of her mounting aggravation as she had to begin each sand castle all over again, day after day.

"I know this sounds silly so please don't laugh, but I believe...I truly believe that there is magic there in each sand castle. I believe in that with my entire heart and maybe, just maybe I will get some of that too. Just a little bit of that."

She explained shyly without facing him. Blade smiled when he realized how vulnerable she had become all of a sudden.

"Some magic? What kind of magic are you wishing for?"

Scarlett hesitated for a moment when she realized how ridiculous she was about to sound. She turned to face him while she was desperate to find the words to make him understand that her sand castles were her key to a brand-new life, "I don't know? I just think there is more to life. More than this; more than Carmel and more than just being Pastor Joe's daughter. I think that whatever it is, it might just sweep me away from here someday, like maybe rescue me, you know?"

She was convinced that she was making no sense at all.

"Rescue you? Do you need rescuing, Scarlett?"

Blade frowned as he wondered why Scarlett was convinced that she needed rescuing.

"I mean, my dad, you know? He can be exactly like an army general sometimes …"

Scarlett became silent at once. Blade nodded his head and gazed back out over Carmel.

"Well, you know? Technically, I rescued you tonight, does that count?" They both erupted into laughter, and it was at that very moment that Blade discovered her remarkable smile.

He stared at her in absolute conjecture while he was unable to take his eyes off her. In one moment, she had turned his rock-solid heart into an unexpected tremble. He had no way of understanding the emotions that had begun to overwhelm him. In his entire life, Blade Bannister had no desire or willful intention of attaching himself to another woman.

He was devotedly sensitive to the authenticity that his father drank himself to death shortly after his mother passed away, and the utter destruction her death had so carelessly left behind, was one that Blade swore he would steer clear of, at any cost. He swore to himself that he would in no way at all, devote himself so entirely to another human being and risk the veracity that she could be abruptly ripped away from him at any moment.

"So, I've never seen you at Church, or anywhere

actually?"

Scarlett had become curious and had a sudden, yet inexplicable urge to discover more about the boy on the motorcycle.

"Yeah, I don't really go to Church. I don't buy into any of that crap anymore."

"You don't believe in God?"

Scarlett was horrified to consider the reality that Blade was a non-believer.

"No, I do. I believe in God, I just don't believe in religion. I don't follow religion of any sort."

"Is there a difference? Is it not one and the same?"

Scarlett was utterly confused by his baffling explanation.

"Yes, there is an enormous difference. I believe in God, Jesus and the Holy Spirit. I don't believe in Churches and Pastors. Many are religious Scarlett, but few are right with God. I find religious people to be boastful and arrogant."

His response was simple, yet entirely sensible which Scarlett understood straight away.

"Yeah, I guess there is a huge difference, just look at Pastor Joe."

She whispered as she thought back to Pastor Joe and his many, perverse rules.

Scarlett glanced at her wristwatch and turned to Blade at once.

"Would you drive me home, please? It's getting so late."

"Sure."

Blade rose to his feet and held out his hand to help her up before he handed her the helmet.

"Drop me a block from my house, my father can't hear your motorcycle." "Alright."

She climbed onto the motorcycle behind him, and once again, she held him firmly around his waist.

The motorcycle came to an abrupt halt only a block away from her home. She hurriedly leaped from the motorcycle and handed him the helmet at once.

"Thank you for tonight. And for rescuing me."

She let out a faint giggle before she whispered excitedly

and hurriedly turned to leave.

"Wait!" He hollered out to her, before she disappeared around the corner. Scarlett turned back to face him while an unintentional, yet tremendous smile had instantly appeared on her face.

"Can I see you again?"

Scarlett moved closer to him as her hands began to tremble,

"I would really like that, a lot but my dad … you know?"

He lowered his head while Scarlett stood staring at him.

"Who knows? Maybe we run into each other again? I hope so! Perhaps you could rescue me again one more time."

Scarlett hurriedly, yet softly climbed up the trellis into her bedroom. When she slid into her bed, she lay staring at the ceiling while recalling her night of absolute rebellion with a boy she had only just met but was attracted to instantly.

She was instantaneously addicted to the emotions of freedom and joy that had made its way into her heart; she was certain that she could hear the hammering of her heart. She could barely suppose that she had defied Pastor Joe and ran off to a night club with Alethea.

She had no intention of meeting a boy, yet Blade was the exact kind of man she dreamed she would meet someday. Her heart began to hammer loudly as she thought back to the ride on the motorcycle and she was assured that it was something she would aspire to relive over and over again.

Blade Bannister was a drifter who found a home and sense of belonging with the "Swift as a Tiger" gang. He was born into dire, yet recent poverty. His mother, Kikki Bannister passed away at childbirth leaving him to be raised by only his father, Bobby who drank himself to death when Blade was merely five years old. Blade was bounced from foster home to foster home before he ran off and was then taken in by Long John Mackenzie.

He taught Blade to earn his keep by repairing motorcycles and cars, and shortly after his twenty first birthday, Long John Mackenzie gifted him with his very own motorcycle that came with a customized leather jacket which signified his initiation into their four-man motorcycle gang.

As he once again rushed through the streets of Carmel, Blade was yet again aware of the unexpected emotions that were building up inside him that were solely brought on by Scarlett. He had never before felt the way he felt when Scarlett wrapped her arms around him while seated behind him on the motorcycle.

Blade was utterly bewildered, but at the same time, he was entirely horrified by the reality that the Pastor's daughter had awoken feelings inside of him he was sure had in no way at all, existed before.

## THE REBELLION

Scarlett rushed down stairs for a hurried breakfast while the events of the previous night had remained fresh and unsullied on her mind. She was powerless to swab the lingering grin from her face, while the image of Pastor Joe could in no way taint the unanticipated elation that had unintentionally crept up on her.

"Good morning, father! Good morning, mother!" She hurriedly slid into an empty seat at the kitchen table while smiling broadly at her parents.

"Are you feeling all right, Scarlett Rose?"

Pastor Joe glared at his daughter while panic and fear had at once made its way into his rigid heart. He was in no way equipped to deal with Scarlett's sudden change in disposition and at once, he glared questioningly at Lily.

"Fine, sir." She responded with an even broader smile.

"Scarlett, are you sure you are alright?"

Lily too, was caught off guard by her daughter's obvious, yet unidentified delight.

"I'm good, Ma'am."

Her smile had in no way faded or even begun to subside.

Pastor Joe was by no means proverbial with Scarlett's swift and unanticipated change in temperament. She seemed lighthearted and in high spirits, which disconcerted him at once.

"What will you be doing today, Scarlett Rose?"

"I thought that perhaps I would go down to the beach and build the sand castle again."

"I wish you would just leave it alone. There are so many better ways to spend your time. I just don't understand why you are always at the beach, building those sand castles…day after day."

Pastor Joe snubbed her as he took a sip of his coffee. Scarlett lowered her head while at once aware that simply Pastor Joe possessed the uncanny ability to plummet her from any high she had found herself on,

"I volunteer at the library, father."

"Well, just don't let me catch you in a bathing suit. Will Alethea be joining you?"

He glowered at once.

"No, daddy, I don't think so?"

"I don't like that girl, Scarlett. She severely lacks discipline."

Pastor Joe shook his head in consternation. "The less you surround yourself with girls like her, the better off you will be."

"You don't like anybody, daddy."

Scarlett was horrified when she realized that she had said it out loud. She peered over at Pastor Joe while confronted by immediate disgust that had appeared on his face.

"Scarlett Rose!" Lily almost dropped her fork as she glanced nervously at Pastor Joe.

"Sorry. I didn't mean for it to come out like that."

They sat in silence for a moment before Scarlett turned back to her mother.

"When will Matthew be home, ma'am?" "Only after his finals next month, Scar."

She bowed her head and leisurely continued with her breakfast. Scarlett utterly adored her older brother Matthew and spent many nights crying herself to sleep as she was desperate for him to return home to her. Pastor Joe seemed increasingly vigilant around Matthew, and when he was home, Scarlett enjoyed a vaster amount of independence.

Matthew would regularly persuade Pastor Joe to allow Scarlett to join him at the movies or for leisured walks around Carmel. At Church, Matthew was known as the catch of Carmel, while Scarlett would become annoyed at the girls that shamelessly threw themselves at him.

Even though they would persistently argue as any brother and sister would, Scarlett felt safest when he was home. He played an enormously unique role in her life and it seemed to Scarlett that their home functioned superiorly only when he was around.

Lily too, smiled more often and seemed more relaxed while Pastor Joe seemed kinder and far more contented when Matthew was under their roof. There were moments when Scarlett was certain that her brother unintentionally intimidated and frightened her father, yet he rarely challenged or disobeyed Pastor Joe.

Matthew would remain calm, yet assertive but he would in no way permit Pastor Joe to oppress him or Scarlett.

Scarlett Rose had barely made her way onto the beach, when she found Alethea waiting for her.

"Oh, thank God you're alright."

She sighed as she snugly embraced Scarlett.

"How did you get home? I was so worried about you! I was looking for you after that whole fight and you were just gone!"

"That guy, Blade, brought me home on his motorcycle after that huge commotion."

Alethea glowered as she smiled broadly at Scarlett. "I saw him, he is so cute!"

Alethea giggled as Scarlett hurriedly gathered the sea sand.

"I don't get you? Each day you build a new sand castle, and each night the tide washes them out? When are you going to quit?"

"Never. Or at least, the day that they are sturdy enough

to withstand the ocean. That'll be the day they light up too, you'll see. Besides, what else am I going to do?"

"So, tell me about that biker dude!"

Alethea was keen to learn all there was to know about Blade Bannister. Scarlett sat back and smiled timidly.

"We spent about an hour together on the hilltop just talking and not talking. He's nice. I like him."

She whispered as she glanced around, afraid that someone might hear her.

"But as you know, Pastor Joe will have none of it, so I probably won't see him again. I mean...who would want to date Pastor Joe's daughter anyways."

"Yeah, I guess, but he can't keep you holed up forever, Scar! Anyways, good luck with your sand castle! I'm headed out to the mall with my mother!"

"Have fun!" Scarlett waved as Alethea sprinted up the path towards her home.

Scarlett intensely envied and desperately hunted the freedom and independence that Alethea had so often taken for granted. Her parents were far more unperturbed by Alethea's comings and goings than Scarlett's parents were.

Pastor Joe was unyielding by the fact that his daughter was not to be exposed to any earthly pleasures or covetousness. It was imperative to preserve an influential and prominent position in Carmel; it was essential that Scarlett and Matthew advocate and exude their proper and appropriate upbringing.

Appearances seemed to be the most important aspect for Pastor Joe and he cringed at the very notion that there would be whispers amongst the members of the community that they were anything but the perfect Christian family.

As Scarlett was frantically building her sand castle, she secretly made plans for the day that she could run off and escape from her father and the town of Carmel.

Ever since she was only a little girl, she decided that someday she would place a tremendous amount of distance between her and Pastor Joe; an enormous amount of time between them so that he could never find her.

At times, the very idea scared her almost to death, but mostly, she would feel excitement build up inside of her as she patiently lingered and anxiously waited for the day to present itself to her. Scarlett often questioned whether she would long for and yearn for her father, but each time, she realized that the very thought of freedom clouded any sense of belonging to the Horak family.

"Scarlett! Scarlett Rose!"

She turned around to find her mother rapidly approaching her. Scarlett rose to her feet and stared skeptically at Lily. "

Your father says for you to come home. We have to clean the Church before tomorrow's service and it's your turn to place fresh flowers on the altar."

"All right, mom. I'll be right there."

The beach was barely a five-minute walk from their home and when Scarlett glanced at her wristwatch, she discovered that it had just turned three in the afternoon. She hurriedly built her barricade around the sandcastle, before she stood up and admired her beautiful, hand crafted mansion in the sand.

"Don't wash away, all right? I'll be back tomorrow." She whispered before she turned to make her way up the path that led home.

When she reached their home, Pastor Joe was anxiously awaiting her return as he apprehensively sat in his old blue Ford Chevy.

Scarlett swiftly made her way into the garden, and gathered a bunch of roses, lilies and daffodils for her altar display. Lily had climbed into the Ford and at once signaled for Scarlett to scurry. Scarlett had just slipped into the backseat, when Pastor Joe turned to her,

"You have the schedule Scarlett, why did your mother have to call for you?"

"Sorry Pastor Joe, I lost track of the time."

"Well, don't let that happen again. Your priorities seem a little distorted lately."

"Yes, sir. It won't happen again."

Scarlett replied despondently as she gazed at the flowers in her hands. She at once thought back to Blade, and she wondered whether she would ever see him again. She was convinced that in no way at all, would any boy aspire to voluntarily rendezvous with Pastor Joe's daughter.

She was keenly aware of the fact that boys found him

intimidating, but mostly, they all feared Pastor Joe as though he was their God and God to Carmel.

From the time that she could accurately recall, Pastor Joe had regularly instructed her to steer clear from any boy other than her brother. He was adamant that they were reckless and sought only the physical pleasures from any young woman.

He was adamant the she by no means at all, maintain or seek out friendships from the opposite sex. Pastor Joe had on countless occasions imprinted the fact that boys' solitary motivation was to taint her soul and distort her body.

He made it clear that should the time come, he and Lily would find an appropriate suitor for her and he frenetically impressed upon Scarlett that his blessing and that of the Church was imperative once a union was to be created.

When her first cycle showed up, Pastor Joe became livid by her bodily filth and refused her access to communion during her so-called phase. Pastor Joe was of the opinion that Scarlett be kept in isolation during her period of impurity and even then, Scarlett Rose never once considered opposing her father's wishes, until she had met Blade Bannister during her one night of rebellion.

She hastily arranged the flowers in the century old Church vase before she placed them on the altar while Lily swept and dusted the Church benches.

Pastor Joe had placed his Scripture on the altar and began rehearsing his sermon for the following morning. Scarlett slid into one of the benches, and in adoration, she listens attentively to her father sermonize.

She had for all time been fascinated by his tenor, yet it was his aptitude in which he carried The Word over that entirely captivated her.

She would regularly question the Scripture, but she would by no means at all, question her father. In Scarlett's mind, he had become God; not only to her but to the entire Carmel village.

His word was of utmost importance to all, and disobeying him was on no account at all, an acceptable or satisfactory option. The town's folk would naturally approach Pastor Joe when any and all decisions were to be made whether minor of enormous significance.

The powerful manner in which he would condemn or put the boot in against any new development, would more often than not, leave the inhabitants of Carmel reeling.

Prior to Christmas a few years back, Mayor Wells approached Pastor Joe to declare the frozen dam an ice-skating zone for the youngsters of Carmel.

Pastor Joe was horrified at the mere suggestion of a social gathering and at once, discarded the proposal as ridiculous and evil. Yet, as Scarlett sat in silence on the Church bench while listening to him, she could barely consider his unreserved divergence from the rest of the world.

There were times that Scarlett was certain that he was, in fact, the prince of darkness as she reminded herself that satan too, was once an angel. She nudged herself of the reality that Pastor Joe was disguised as a man of God as he gathered his flock and led them onto a path of eternal damnation.

For as long as Scarlett could recall, she was susceptible to an overwhelming, yet gently voice inside of her that prodded her to remain firm and unrelenting in her own beliefs.

There was something supernatural inside of and around her that Scarlett was certain was lunging at her to discover the truth about the Gospel and about Pastor Joe.

When her father acted out in desperation and frustration

at the distorted souls of Carmel, she would once again be alert to the jolt from the innermost part of her, while she grew increasingly uncomfortable and unimpressed around Pastor Joe.

Other than emotions of torment and fear, she was convinced that something superior was breathing inside of her and that she should remain steadfast in her innermost struggle with him.

When they pulled into the driveway of their home, Scarlett smiled when she noticed that the stars of the night had come out in all their magnificence. They had barely arrived and made their way indoors when there was a faint thud on their front door.

Scarlett and Lily were setting the dinner plates while Pastor Joe had sat contentedly in his chair directly across the fire place as he habitually studied the Scripture. Pastor Joe swiftly glanced at the clock against the wall when he exasperatingly made his way to the front door. "Yes?" He at once noticed a young man appearing bewildered and anxious.

"Hi. Is Scarlett home?"

Scarlett at once recognized Blade's voice while sudden terror made its way into her heart. She was certain that her lungs were being clasped into a bare set of hands while they were tightening their grip around them.

"Oh no. Blade. Why did he come here?" She thought apprehensively while uncertain of how to act in response or precisely, how to give an explanation of him, to her father.

"Scarlett? You're looking for Scarlett Rose Horak?" Pastor Joe frowned in anger at once.

"Yes sir." Blade responded in hesitation as he became anxious all of a sudden.

"Come inside." Pastor Joe hesitated for a moment before he made way for Blade to enter his home.

"Scarlett!"

He called out to her while Lily became restless at once. She was immensely fearful of Pastor Joe's reception to a strange boy in their home while he sternly prohibited Scarlett from any form of contact with any boy other than Matthew.

She was desperately terrified of his wrath while she was fearful of the indubitable vehemence he would inflict upon Scarlett.

"Yes, daddy?"

Scarlett at once appeared by her father's side.

"Do you know this young man?"

He glared at her with abrupt antagonism and resentment.

"Yes, sir. We've, we've only met once, daddy."

"Have a seat then, young man."

Pastor Joe signaled to an empty sofa in the living room. Blade hesitantly and anxiously made his way over to the empty seat while devastatingly convinced that he had instantly placed Scarlett in an uncompromising position.

Pastor Joe and Scarlett followed shortly behind him where Pastor Joe had returned to his seat and Scarlett making her way to an empty seat directly across from Blade.

Pastor Joe held his index finger, along with his middle finger against his temple as he glared irately at Blade. Scarlett had become immensely uncomfortable while the strain of her father's mannerism was evident on her face.

"I am Blade, Blade Bannister." Blade got up from his seat in a desperate attempt to offer his extended hand out to Pastor Joe. Pastor Joe hesitantly shook his hand before Blade reluctantly returned to his seat.

Pastor Joe was at once staggered by the unexpected introduction and unmistakable recognition of his last name. He was noticeably dishonored by his daughter's blatant disobedience and utterly horrified by the fact that she had met a Bannister.

"Bannister, huh? Are you any relation to Kikki and Bobby Bannister?" Pastor Joe leaned forward as he closed the Scripture before he placed it on the coffee table beside him.

"Yes sir, they were my parents."

His voice had begun to shudder at once while he was unsure and entirely confused by the fact that Pastor Joe recognized and referred to his parents who had been deceased for the majority of sixteen years. Pastor Joe was compelled to remain calm in a desperate attempt to manipulate the aggression that had begun building up inside of him.

He leaned back into his seat, but by the expression on his face, Scarlett was convinced that her father in no way approved of their unexpected meeting.

"Where did you meet this young man, Scarlett?"

Scarlett was distinctly certain that he was disconcerted while his demeanor had become tempestuous and abrupt.

"I, we met ..." Her voice was shuddering as she thought back to the night that she had unintentionally met Blade Bannister, but before she could come about with a reasonable and acceptable explanation of their meeting, Blade calmly interrupted her as she was about to continue.

"At school sir. Mrs. Johnson's car broke down and I had to tow it in. Scarlett was helping Mrs. Johnson unload her car." He lied as soon as he realized that Scarlett had become distressed and panicky all of a sudden.

From where he was seated, he noticed her quivering hands and her face that had turned ashen.

She was at once relieved by his version of events, even though it was a lie, yet she could in no way at all risk Pastor Joe discovering the one night that she so carelessly snuck out of their house. Blade at once noticed her relief and smiled bashfully before he turned back to Pastor Joe.

"Scarlett Rose, go help your mother with dinner."

Pastor Joe's annoyance and anger had grown, and as he rose to his feet, he turned to Blade.

"Let's take a walk."

Blade got up from the sofa before Pastor Joe led the way out through the front door. Scarlett had become visibly shaken by Pastor Joe's suggestion while she was overwhelmed by an odd premonition that the night would end ghastly.

She feared for Blade and she feared her father's wrath. Scarlett was staggered that Blade had showed up entirely without warning and as she made her way into the kitchen, she was keenly aware of a hollow sensation that had found its way into the pit of her stomach.

She was powerless to defend or protect Blade from Pastor Joe, yet she was desperate for Blade to escape his fury and to never return to their home or to her.

"How could you, Scar?" Her mother stared accusingly at her while at the same time, she immensely feared for her daughter.

"I didn't know he would show up, mother. I only met him once."

"You are not to cavort with boys, Scarlett, you know that?" Lily snapped as she began placing the knives and forks on the dinner table.

"I am not cavorting mama. That's not fair, I'm not permitted to have any friends or go anywhere. All the other girls have computers and mobile phones and are allowed to go out and have fun. All dad let's me do is go down to the beach or to Church!" Scarlett became tensely defensive at once.

"You will not defy your father, Scarlett. You will obey him. The Good Lord will not look fondly upon your behavior!"

Lily was desperate for her daughter to appreciate that she in no way at all, refuse to comply with Pastor Joe's rules.

"Mama! Just stop with all the Good Lord bullshit! I take it from Pastor Joe, but you? I am a good Christian girl; I behave just as you and father expect me to.

I never question you and I never go against father's wishes. This was one time, mama. I am seventeen years old! It's not fair! Don't bring the Good Lord into this. The Good Lord doesn't work like this, mama!"

Scarlett Rose had reached breaking point as she reflected on all that she had worked towards while frantic to become the ideal daughter. She was exhausted of maintaining an acceptable image to society and she was tired Pastor Joe's unreasonable rules.

"Scarlett Rose! Mind your language! As long as you are under your father's roof, you will do as he says! Every single time, do you understand me?"

Lily was overcome with fear as she witnessed her daughter's sudden outbreak of insurgence.

"I don't want to be here, mama. I don't want to be under this roof. I can't wait to leave and never come back!" She bellowed out through the tears that had begun to roll down her cheeks.

"Scarlett, don't speak like that." Lily was overcome with dejection as she heard the despondency in her daughter's voice.

"What do you think they're talking about right now, mama? Right at this very minute? Pastor Joe isn't getting to know him. You know as well as I do that he is putting the fear of God into him! No man would want me because of Pastor Joe and I don't want a man that he chooses. I like Blade, mama!"

Scarlett became hysterical at the mere thought that at that very moment, Pastor Joe was threatening Blade. Lily lowered her head and continued to set the dinner table.

"I am never going to meet somebody I like! Pastor Joe will scare all the boys away!"

Alice VL – Zandri Burger

"Scarlett, hush now."

Lily placed her hand on Scarlett's shoulder while Scarlett hurriedly swabbed at the tears that were rolling unreservedly down her cheeks.

Pastor Joe and Blade Barrington walked side by side in silence up the path to the river until they reached the old and only windmill that was left in Carmel. Blade nervously glared at Pastor Joe who stood staring at the historic windmill in an eerie silence.

"My daughter … she's a good Christian girl. She is somebody, she is important, and she is a Horak."

Blade was instantly confused as he stood staring at Pastor Joe.

"The Bannisters and the Horaks have never seen eye to eye. A thousand years would pass before a Horak and a Bannister would walk together. A mistake like this was made a hundred years before and I won't let something like that happen again. Do you understand?

Do you know anything of your history, boy? I don't want you to see Scarlett again. I won't allow it. Not even over my dead body."

Pastor Joe gazed confidently at Blade.

"Pastor Joe, I don't know anything about our family's history with yours, but I am not a bad person. Shouldn't Scarlett decide?"

"Scarlett doesn't know what she wants. I am her father and I know what's good for her. You come from nothing, you have nothing. What can you ever offer my daughter? What kind of a life will she have with you? You are poor. You have nothing, boy." Pastor Joe became infuriated at once.

"I might come from poverty, Pastor Joe but I am hard working. I will work as hard as it takes to take care of Scarlett if it ever came down to that. We've only just met once and you're making it sound as though I am proposing? She can make her own decisions. You can't decide for her."

"Is that what you think? Really? I am her father. She does not know your history like I do. She has no idea who you are or where you come from? Do you really think Scarlett is your equal? She is better than you."

"You can't hold me accountable for whatever bad blood there is between you and my family? I don't even know what you are talking about!" Blade became agitated almost immediately.

The Weeping Prince & The Mansion in Sand

"I will do what I have to, to protect my daughter from you, Bannister. Whatever it takes and whatever I deem necessary."

"Protect her from what? From me?"

Pastor Joe knelt down and grabbed a chunk of muddy grime in his hands, "See this, this was our land. Our blood and sweat flows into this land. Hundreds of years ago, we defended what was ours however was necessary. Make no mistake, I will defend that which is mine with the same vigor."

Blade stood staring at Pastor Joe, unable to make sense of what he was saying.

"I don't understand, you think you need to defend Scarlett from me? I have no idea where your land comes into this? I will never hurt her, so I don't understand why you feel the need to defend her from me?"

"From you and your kind, yes."

"My kind? I'm not going to hurt her."

"That's not what I am worried about; I don't want her mingling with your sort."

Pastor Joe shook his hand as the mud fell to the ground

before he moved closer to Blade.

"You are to leave Scarlett alone. Leave Carmel. You don't belong here. You don't belong in Carmel...you never have."

Blade lowered his head while staring at the ground. Pastor Joe was blatantly banishing him from Carmel, and all he could think of was Scarlett.

At that very moment, Blade Bannister knew that no matter how threatened he felt in front of Pastor Joe at that very moment or at any other moment, he had no intention of leaving Scarlett Horak behind.

"You will not drive me out. You cannot. You call yourself a Pastor? I am going nowhere." Blade turned away from Pastor Joe and hurriedly made his way back towards the village.

When Pastor Joe returned home without Blade barely an hour later, Scarlett noticed that he seemed disheveled and entirely conquered.

He seemed to have aged ten years in the short hour which made way for feelings of shame that had begun to overwhelm Scarlett.

Pastor Joe frantically made his way into the kitchen

where he hurriedly scrubbed his hands. He washed and scrubbed vigorously in an attempt to clean the grit and the grime that had settled in between his fingers and under his nails. As soon as he had dried his hands, Pastor Joe turned to Scarlett who was seated beside Lily at the kitchen table.

"You are never to see that boy again, Scarlett. Never. I forbid it."

He was fiercely rigid as he commanded her to steer clear form Blade Bannister.

"You shouldn't be cavorting with any boys at your age, let alone the Bannister boy!"

He raised his shuddering voice while he was overcome with tremendous anger and resentment.

"Why not? You can't forbid me!" Scarlett pushed her chair aside as she rose to her feet.

"Oh, yes I can, and because I said so! And since when do you question any of my commands?"

"No father, no! Since now. I am a good girl. I do well at school. I am always at home! I go to Church almost every day and I teach Sunday School every Sunday. I never question your

# The Weeping Prince & The Mansion in Sand

authority, but I like him, and I want to see him again! You have never had faith in me! You and mom don't trust me, and I have never, ever given you a reason to distrust me. Never, father, never!"

Scarlett hollered at the top of her voice before Pastor Joe reached out and aggressively struck her across her face. Scarlett staggered slightly and was horrified that he had clouted her. In all of her seventeen years, he had never lifted one hand out of anger towards her.

Scarlett was aware of a burning sensation that had made its way onto her cheek, and as she desperately attempted to gulp back on her tears, she realized that there was no way that she could stop her tears from rolling disconsolately down her cheeks.

"He is a Bannister, Scarlett! He comes from the wrong side of the tracks and is not good enough for you! Do you know what he does for a living? He fixes other people's cars. Rich people's cars, Scarlett, like us. He recklessly drives a motorcycle and has no family. He has no history, no heritage and absolutely no class. You will not go against my wishes!"

Pastor Joe's face had turned a bright red as his antagonism escalated.

"There has been bad blood between the Bannister and Horak clans for hundreds of years. A feud that was born in the 1800's. Your union with a Bannister will not take place. You will not defy my wishes; do you understand me?"

He grabbed a hold of her arm and tightened his grip at once. Scarlett was excruciatingly attentive of her tears that were flowing unreservedly down her cheeks. At that very moment, Scarlett loathed her father, Pastor Joe, a man of God.

His piercing blue eyes had turned almost arctic as he glared at her in utter fury. For an instant, Scarlett was certain that she was face to face with satan himself. That familiar and nudging little voice inside of her, prodded her once again to stand strong and to remain firm.

"Go to your room, Scarlett. We'll ask forgiveness for your sins tomorrow in Church." He ordered her to leave the kitchen at once, while Lily had anxiously begun serving supper.

When he sat down at the kitchen table, Lily was reeling from his unexpected outburst and the predictable conflict that had taken place between father and daughter only moments before. She felt immense pity for Scarlett, yet she was keenly aware of the confrontation between the two families dating back to more than two hundred years.

She was convinced that Pastor Joe would in no way at all bless any union between Scarlett and another man, let alone a Bannister.

"You can't keep her caged like this, Joseph."

Lily raucously whispered as she glared at her husband.

"For as long as she is under this roof, she will do as I say."

Pastor Joe was unyielding in his decision.

"Besides, the boy has left town. Why can't she befriend a boy like Carter Jethro?"

"The heart wants what the heart wants, Joseph. You know that?"

Lily was anxious for her husband to loosen his grip over Scarlett.

"Remember when we began dating?"

"Lily Horak, our families came together and blessed our union once the Church had agreed to our joining together."

"Joseph, are you saying that had we not reserved the Church or the families' blessings, we would not have wed?"

"That's precisely what I am saying, Lily."

Lily was horrified by his sudden revelation and unexpected admission. She had always considered their union as sacred; as a coming together by preference and by love.

In all the years, she had attributed his aloofness to his love of God, and in no way at all, ever considered the fact that there was no real love or adoration between them.

Lily adored Joseph from the moment she had met him at Church Camp. She thought him to be highly intelligent and incredibly charming.

His love of God and his devotion to the Church was precisely what attracted her to him right from the start. Lily was horrified to discover that Joseph Horak was barely as dedicated to her, as she was to him.

"Do you love me, Joseph? I mean...did you ever love me?"

Pastor Joe turned to face Lily before he abruptly lowered his head.

"There is no such thing, Lily. It's about what works. You work for me, and I for you. This is what God wanted."

While she took a seat beside him, her heart had begun to shatter into a thousand fractions. She was aware of a confining lump in her throat while her tears were brimming in her eyes. At that very instant, Lily was convinced that she was no better than a common traitor; she had in no way at all stood up for Scarlett out of respect and love for Joseph.

Her daughter's heart was crushed by the parents that should shield her from harm and pain. Lily had no clue as to how to mend her relationship with her little girl once again. She had taken Pastor Joe, her husband's side too often. The innermost part of her had often nudged her to hear Scarlett and to listen more closely, yet she continued to favor Pastor Joe and his unreasonable authority.

"I want Scarlett to love, Joseph. It shouldn't matter who he is or where he's from, if she loves him, I want to support her. I want her to be happy. I don't want this for her." Lily wiped a single tear that had abruptly rolled from her eye.

"It does matter, Lily. What is love? It's purely infatuation. The only love that lives inside of us is our love of God. There is no other love. We have a responsibility towards Scarlett and to God to keep her out of the clutches of the dark souls that surround us. We will not discuss this again, are we clear?"

Pastor Joe stomped his fist onto the dining room table before Lily bowed her head in devastation.

Scarlett collapsed onto her bed and sobbed violently into her pillow by the mere thought of never seeing Blade again. For the first time in her life, she had met a boy that she truly felt familiar and at ease with. He had evolved into her knight in shining armor when he rescued her from an intimidating drunk in The Doll's House; a man she was certain that her mansion in the sand would perhaps someday send her.

She had come alive again and she had begun to look forward to her tomorrows. Other than her sand castles, Blade Bannister was responsible for the immense joy and contentment that was building up inside of her.

"There has to be more. This can't be all there is. There must be more. Dear God, there must be more for me." Scarlett pleaded while weeping ferociously into her pillow.

# BANNISTER VS HORAK
## THE FEUD

In the early 1800's, Carmel was once merely known as a blooming and bustling farming community. The Bannister and Horak families were both livestock ranchers, although the Bannisters planted additional maize and sunflower crops.

The Bannister family had owned land alongside the interconnecting river that ran from the ocean for hundreds of miles inland. On the direct opposite side of their farm, the Horak clan had owned their own vast acres of land.

Before 1860, both families were in actuality great friends and would often attend one another's social gatherings while Sundays were reserved for the getting-together of the two families. Minor discrepancies and accusations such as pilfering cattle from one another had escalated over a number of years which failed to recognize neither of the families as a pillar in the farming community.

Their falling out occurred roughly around 1860 while legend has it that it had originally begun when the Bannisters accused the Horaks of thieving their cattle from them. At the time, there were minor confrontations which usually led to fist-fighting or name-calling, but nothing more.

When the Horak family had sold their farm to developers hoping to turn the land into a town by building houses and shopping malls, the Bannisters were unwilling to surrender and remained firm and adamant to retain their farm and surrounding lands.

To add insult to injury, Rory Bannister had fallen in love with Catherine Horak, the daughter of the Clan leader, Raymond Horak. Shortly after their first meeting, Rory had claimed her as his bride in the midst of their exhausting and on-going rivalry and scuffles.

Barely seven months into their marriage, Catherine gave birth to Roger Bannister who would be their only child. This utterly devastated the Horak family and resulted in the fact that they entirely discarded the bloodline between the two families while they would regularly refer to Roger as a bastard son.

For years, the Horaks had engaged in warfare with the Bannisters in a desperate attempt to split the union and to compel the family to sell their land. The Horaks had joined forces with the Jethro clan and had established the Jethro-Horak

Development Company in a desperate attempt to profit from modern day society while the Bannisters had remained unfaltering on their land which was preventing the further development of Carmel.

As the years had progressed, developing the town that would be known as Carmel, had come to an abrupt halt when it became clear that the Bannisters were in no way prepared to surrender their land or to return Catherine to the Horak family. In the early 1860's, a severe fire had destroyed the crops and the cattle on the Bannister ranch, almost engulfing the entire farmland, barns and colonial home. As they unsuccessfully attempted to rebuild their farm, the bank foreclosed on their loans which were used entirely to rebuild their farm and forced them from the same land they had owned for hundreds of years.

Raymond Bannister was convinced that the Horaks were responsible for the utter devastation and vowed to remain in conflict with the entire Horak family from that day forward.

After losing their lands, and in utter desperation, Raymond Horak struck Catherine Horak in a fit of unsolicited anger, leaving Rory Bannister frantic to defend and protect his wife.

The feud brewing between the two families had ended in

tragedy when Catherine flung herself, together with Roger into the river from the cliff, behind the only remaining barn in Carmel.

Upon hearing of Catherine's death, Edward Bannister, Rory's father had arranged a meeting with Raymond Horak in an attempt to settle the feud for once and for all. Once Edward realized that there was to be no settling of a hundred-year-old feud, he turned his back on Raymond to simply walk away from the Horak clan. Raymond drew his revolver that he had persistently carried around with him, and fatally shot Edward in the back.

In retaliation, Rory Bannister disfigured Raymond Horak's face when he lured him into the barn and overpowered him. Raymond had died within days from sepsis when it was discovered that Rory had used a contaminated and rusted knife blade.

Shortly after Raymond's death, the two families went their separate ways after vowing to remain distant and in opposition from one another from that day forward. Rory had met Charlene Johnson shortly after they were banished from their lands and reluctantly settled into Carmel with the remainder of the Bannister clan.

Rory and Charlene were married for a little over a year

when they welcomed their son Bobby into the world. Shortly before Bobby turned six, Charlene passed away after a short battle with small pox.

Rory Bannister and his son, Bobby Bannister swore to seek retribution on the Horak clan for their contribution to the fire that had left them homeless and penniless, but when Rory passed away suddenly due to a fragile heart, Bobby's only concern was to lay the feud to rest while he refused to linger in rage.

He was convinced that an excessive and unnecessary amount of bloodshed had taken place between the two families and he vowed that he would detach himself from the entire warfare.

He had met Kikki at the young age of eighteen, and with only his job at the railroad to support them, they had moved into an old, dilapidated railroad house at what was known as the wrong side of the tracks.

As Carmel had begun to thrive and develop, it was more significant than ever for Bobby to distance himself from the entire Horak clan. They were left poor and desolate after the entire family fortune had burnt to the ground along with their home, crops and cattle.

From a distance, Bobby Bannister witnessed Carmel's growth as the flourishing town regularly reminded him of his family's heritage that was lost to him and his offspring for all eternity.

He would become angry at times when he witnessed the Horak's prosperity in Carmel and it blinded him with rage that Joseph Horak was appointed Pastor of the only Church in the village; the same Church Joseph Horak had built.

When Kikki passed away at childbirth, Bobby was desperate to mend fences with the only surviving Horak and Pastor to their town. Bobby Bannister had met Pastor Joe in Church late one Sunday afternoon only hours before the evening service.

He was desperate to put an end to the fighting between the two families and he was hopeful that his son, Blade would be accepted into the community, and perhaps attend Church on a Sunday along with the other children of Carmel.

He pleaded with Pastor Joe to realize and observe that he was losing sight of his humanity and that they were wasting precious time by distinguishing between social classes. Pastor Joseph Horak was a stubborn man; he was devotedly sensitive to their history and the bad blood between the Horak and Bannister families that went back many years.

As was passed down by his father and his father before him, Pastor Joe was convinced that Bobby Bannister's bloodline had been tainted. He refused to accept a desperate plea for peace and informed Bobby that Carmel had no room whatsoever for peasants.

He dismissed Bobby at once and ordered him to leave the Church and to never return. The feud had remained animate, glowing and unending, much to Bobby Bannister's consternation.

"Joseph, we had no part in this. Why do you choose to carry this around with you? We are cut from the same cloth."

Bobby Bannister was desperate to make sense of Pastor Joe's inability to move forward.

"We are not cut from the same cloth. Our fathers and our fathers before that is to be honored, or else it would all have been for nothing! Your father's first wife was a Horak! Because of the Bannisters, she took her and her son's life!"

"We all have different versions, Joseph. All I want is for my boy to come to Church."

"I can't refuse him, but he wouldn't fit in here."

Pastor Joe was adamant to keep Bobby and Blade Bannister out of his Church.

# THE LIBERATION OF SCARLETT ROSE

Scarlett Rose made her way to an isolated bench in her father's Church the following morning. Her eyes were red and distended as she stared straight ahead of her. She was barred from participating in the choir that morning, and while she listened to her mother's piercing voice, she was confined by a restricting lump in her throat.

She had barely slept a wink the previous night as she refused to accept that she was to discard Blade Bannister. She felt sick to her stomach by the mere thought of never seeing him stand in front of her again, and it scared her tremendously that she had developed enormous, yet unexplained feelings for him.

Her heart began to pounce when she thought back to his emerald green eyes and her legs grew weak when she recalled his gigantic smile.

As the choir became silent, she noticed her father hurriedly make his way to the altar. He walked upright and proudly, and when he reached the altar, he turned around to face his faithful congregation in all his splendor and magnificence. She glared at him in acrimony as she listened to him welcome all his parishioners, while thanking the choir for their beautiful rendition of 'The rock that is higher than I.'

Scarlett had always been keenly enthusiastic about the hymns the choir would lead the service with, but at that very moment, she observed all members of his flock as absolute hypocrites, including her beloved mother, Lily.

As Pastor Joe began his sermon, Scarlett's mind drifted back to Blade. She thought back to the previous night and was once again horrified by Pastor Joe's shunning of Blade. She recalled Pastor Joe violently striking her, and she was agonizingly aware of the unreserved condescension that had welled up inside of her. The restricting lump in her throat had grown larger while her tears were rolling unreservedly from her eyes.

When she turned her attentiveness back to his sermon, she heard him advocate love, humility and acceptance. He loudly exclaimed that no one person was dissimilar in the eyes of the Lord.

She heard him command that human beings were children of the King and that they were all equivalent, irrespective of ethnicity, wealth and color. Pastor Joe was adamant that God in no way distinguished between affluence and poverty and that all were identical in His eyes.

"No one burial hole was any different irrespective of wealth or power. God does in no way at all distinguish between earthly stature and He by no means whatsoever, adjudicates His children by their worldly achievements. We shall love our neighbors, brothers and sisters, precisely as we love ourselves."

Scarlett was appalled and sickened by his phony sermon. Once more, she was certain that satan was actively toiling through her father, the beloved Pastor Joe of Carmel. Only the night before had he informed her of the legitimacy that Blade Bannister was by no means equal to her; he was in fact, below her.

She became irate at once and when she rose to her feet, she was aware of a robotic urge to question her father and his sermon.

She apprehensively, yet incontrovertibly made her way down the aisle as the entire congregation grew silent around her. She gazed straight ahead of her and fixed her eyes firmly on Pastor Joe. "You're a liar, Pastor Joe!"

She bellowed as her father became hushed while she noticed embarrassment and anger on his face. She could hear fellow members of the congregation gasp for air after which she was certain that she could hear a pin drop. She swallowed profusely on the lump in her throat, while dabbing violently at the tears on her cheek.

"You stand there and preach that we are all alike! You speak of burial plots that are of the exact same depth and length, irrespective of culture, wealth or ethnicity. You hypocritically preach that we are equal in the eyes of the Lord, yet only last night you banished a boy from your home simply because he was from the wrong side of the Carmel tracks!"

She paused to take in a deep breath before Pastor Joe furiously interrupted her. "Sit down, Scarlett Rose!"

"I won't sit down and be quiet! You would have to strike me right here, in front of your flock to silence me, just as you did last night! You act as though you are a good Christian man; you portray this image of having the perfect wife and children who firmly stand behind you and obey you, which they do, yet behind closed doors, you condemn us all into an eternity in hell! You banish us for our so-called sins. The only sin we are guilty of, is enforcing our own free will which was given to us by God, and not by you!"

Pastor Joe shot invisible daggers at his daughter, while

the gasps and whispers had escalated amongst the congregation.

"May God forgive your troubled mind and distorted soul, Scarlett Rose." He replied almost in a whisper while he had maintained a fixed glare on her.

"Forgive me? May God forgive *you*. I sit here, day after day and I listen to you sermonizing. I hear you cast judgments upon the good people of Carmel. I listen to you preach the so-called word of God and I hate you for it. I hate you! You are the dark prince with the Scripture in your hands! You are leading all these souls astray due to your unreasonable veiling of our free will. That's not what God wants; God wants us to use our free will while you...you are smothering the citizens of Carmel! You are creating soldiers instead of willing followers!"

She shouted out before she turned and ran from her father's Church. The entire congregation was silenced and utterly staggered by Scarlett Rose's sudden and astonishing outburst. The whispers grew louder as Pastor Joe was desperate to continue with his sermon. Lily stared up at him in utter disgust while listening to members of the Church express sympathy for Scarlett Rose,

"It was only a matter of time, you know?" She heard a faint whisper in a sleeve. "Poor child."

Lily could hear another whisper and when she lowered her head, she suddenly realized that Pastor Joe was not the man she thought she had married.

Scarlett ran down the path away from the Church while desperate to reach the beach. She reflected back on her father's sermon and reminded herself of the downright pretense and double standards that she had been living under for her entire life.

By no means before had she doubted her father, or the sermonizing of Pastor Joe and his beliefs. He had in one moment, distorted her entire confidence in the Church and her religion. She no longer believed in him and she no longer placed any faith in his sermons. While her devotion to her father and her Church slipped away from her, Scarlett no longer felt as though she belonged with him or in Carmel. At that very moment, Scarlett understood the enormous difference between her belief in God and her religion. Blade was right; you can have one without the other.

While kneeling at the spot where her sand castle had been washed away day after day for the past thirteen years, Scarlett was desperate to once again bring her mansion in the sand back to life. While her tears were drowning out her eyes, she desperately and frantically scurried to gather the sea sand.

"Dear God, please forgive me. Please come down here and save me. I have paid my debt to the Church, God, to Pastor Joe. They are all hypocrites, please come down here!" Scarlett shouted at as she stared straight up into the sky.

"Scar? Are you crying?" She was at once aware of Blade's familiar voice beside her.

"Blade? I thought, I thought you left town?"

She leapt to her feet while hurriedly swabbing at her tears.

"I'm here Scar, for you. I'm not going anywhere."

He took her hands into hers and squeezed them firmly.

"I'm so glad you didn't leave. I am so sorry for my father's behavior last night, but it doesn't change anything! Pastor Joe won't let me see you!"

She sorrowfully stumbled over her words as her tears were gushing from her eyes.

"I know, Scar, but I can't walk away from you just like that. I can't. I don't know why but, I don't really want to know either. He doesn't have to know. For some reason, I am stuck here in Carmel. I can't leave. I don't want to leave."

Blade took her into his arms and held her assertively against him.

"I can't let go of you, Blade...I don't want to."

Scarlett felt as though her heart was about to hammer right out of her chest.

"Will you sit here with me for a while?"

"Sure, let's put this sucker back together."

He at once joined Scarlett in gathering enough sea sand in a desperate attempt at rebuilding Scarlett's sand castle. Blade was determined to keep Scarlett's dream alive by one day, building her the sand castle that would be all she had ever hoped it to be. Scarlett gazed at him often in silence while Blade stared at her frequently.

Often, he would smile while she would regularly dab at a lost tear that had rolled down her cheek. When they had been building for almost an hour, Scarlett heard her mother's proverbial voice from a distance. "Scarlett!"

Scarlett turned to face Blade as panic had begun to make

its way into her heart.

"Meet my tonight behind the old barn on the cliff, overlooking the river."

He hurriedly kissed her on the cheek and when Scarlett turned towards her mother, Blade had instantly disappeared into the bushes.

She walked up to her mother while frantically glancing around her, hoping that Lily would in no way at all realize that she had spent the hour with Blade.

"You are to come home at once!"

Lily hollered out to her before she turned back to the path that led right up to their home.

When Scarlett made her way up the stairs to their front porch, she found Pastor Joe seated on a patio chair.

"Come sit down, Scarlett."

He responded sternly when he noticed her ascend the stairs. Scarlett hesitantly made her way to a patio chair directly across from him.

"I discussed this with your mother, and I think we need

to tighten the strings with you. You are completely out of control, Scarlett. I don't know what has gotten into to you? I will not stand by and allow you to speak to me in the way that you did under God's roof. You humiliated me in front of the entire congregation. Do you understand what you have done? Now they think that I'm weak, Scarlett. If a Pastor cannot control and lead his daughter; how could I be expected to manage the entire congregation? No. you are grounded."

He replied calmly, yet sternly.

"You can't control people, father! Grounded from what? What is there to ground me from? I have been grounded since the day I was born!"

She was annoyed with Pastor Joe; she was enraged at his unreasonable demands of her.

"You are no longer to go to the beach unaccompanied, and your mother will walk you to school in the mornings and home in the afternoons. You are no longer to see Alethea Scott, and you will address me with honor and you will show me the respect I deserve."

"You know what, Pastor Joe? I hate you! You don't deserve my respect! You are not an honorable man! Not only do you think you are a man of God, you think you are God!"

Scarlett snapped at him before she hurriedly made her way upstairs into her bedroom. She had barely collapsed onto her bed, when she thought back to Blade Bannister.

At that very moment, she resolved to meet him at the barn on the cliff that night, just as soon as Pastor Joe and Lily were asleep. She would once again, sneak through her bedroom window and scurry down the trellis. Scarlett was certain that there was more to life than simply existing under the command of Pastor Joe.

Her heart nudged her to find a place where she could exist freely and belong unconditionally.

From the innermost part of her, Scarlett knew that there was something beautiful just waiting for her; lingering until the day that she found it.

She wanted to be wonderful and she was desperate for her mere existence to represent something more than the nothingness she had become imprisoned in.

Scarlett dreamed of something spectacular that would brighten up her mere subsistence and she wished for a tomorrow filled with sovereignty and complete happiness. Her heart began to hammer at the mere thought of seeing Blade again, while her entire body was surrounded by the excitement that had begun to overwhelm her.

"Scarlett Rose!" She heard her mother call from the kitchen downstairs. Scarlett hurriedly made her way into the kitchen when she discovered Lily holding the telephone in her hand.

"Your brother wants to speak to you." She handed the receiver to Scarlett at once, before she abruptly turned away and made her way into the living room.

"Matty?" She was ecstatic to hear her brother's comforting voice on the other end of the call.

"Hey Scar. How are you? Pastor Joe says you are a little temperamental? Apparently, you had an outburst in Church this morning?" Matthew chuckled at the unlikely thought.

"I hate him, Matty. I want to run away!" She whispered almost inaudibly.

"I know sissy, but you have to stick it out. You can't have outbursts like that in Church. I know it's hard and I know that Pastor Joe is unreasonable and unfair, but you're just going to make it harder for yourself. If you don't cross him and resolve to just obey him, you'll be fine."

Matthew engaged in a valiant attempt to shield his sister from their father's wrath.

"He struck met, Matty." Scarlett sobbed into the phone while Matthew became irate at once.

"He did? Dad hit you? I'm so sorry, Scar."

"When are you coming home? I just want you to come home!" Scarlett was desperate to see her brother again.

"I'll be home for Christmas, I promise. You'll be eighteen soon, Scar. It's around the corner and then Pastor Joe can no longer keep you there against your will, just follow his rules for a little while longer." He reassured her before he hurriedly said goodbye to his sister.

Scarlett replaced the receiver and when she turned around, she was at once startled to find Lily standing behind her.

"Dinner's almost ready."

Lily brushed past Scarlett on her way to the oven. She was convinced that her mother was eaves-dropping on her conversation with Matthew, but she made no mention of it.

"I'm not hungry." She replied swiftly before she hurried upstairs and made her way back into her bedroom.

"Scarlett Rose!" Pastor Joe's voice echoed through the halls of their colonial home, right into her bedroom while piercing into her ears.

"What now?" She thought as she dejectedly made her way downstairs once again.

"It's Scripture and prayer time. Sit down." He demanded sternly as she appeared before him in the dining room.

"I don't want to." Scarlett remained firm in her sudden rebellion against her father.

"You will sit down and read from the Scripture before you lead the house in prayer tonight."

Pastor Joe hurriedly pulled a chair out and signaled for Scarlett to take a seat.

"I won't." Scarlett refused to sit down as per her father's direct instructions.

"We must pray for you, Scarlett. We must ask God to banish the demons inside of you."

Lily became anxious at once while she was horrified to listen to Pastor Joe demonize their daughter.

"Pray to whom, Pastor Joe? God? Or to you?"

Scarlett shouted out to Pastor Joe before she glanced over at Lily who had become visibly shaken.

"Scarlett Rose, I will whip you if you don't hush at once!" He furiously grabbed her by her arm.

"Why don't you rather strike me, again?" She frenetically attempted to liberate her arm from his grip.

"This is what happens when you fraternize and hobnob with the outside world! You have opened yourself up for satan! You have led him right inside of you and our home, Scarlett."

He released her arm, and disconsolately sat back in his chair while paging through the scripture.

"You don't know who I consort or fraternize with, or if I even do! You haven't even asked me if I had seen Blade Bannister again!

You just assume that I do. I can do nothing right in your eyes and you always, always think the worst of me. I am a good girl, Pastor Joe, I am!" Scarlett bellowed as her tears began to brim in her eyes.

"I don't have to ask you, I've told you, Blade Bannister has left town and he will never return."

He swiftly placed his glasses on his eyes and turned back to the Scripture.

"Scar, sit down, please." Lily desperately urged her while sensing a violent confrontation about to erupt between father and daughter.

"I don't want to. I'm going to bed." She replied matter-of-factly before she sprinted upstairs and returned to her bedroom

# THE BARN

Sunday evenings in Carmel seemed a little frostier to Scarlett than any other evening of the week. It was one month before winter would be in full swing while Scarlett was certain that it would become increasingly challenging as she endeavored to sneak out to meet Blade in the shadows of the night.

She hurriedly sprinted the half mile to the barn, and when she made her way around the back, she found Blade standing on the cliff, silently gazing out over the river. She walked up to him, and gentle touched his shoulder.

"Hey, Scar! I didn't think you'd make it!" He was thrilled and enormously pleased to find her standing beside him.

"I snuck out, again. I wouldn't miss this for anything, not even for Pastor Joe." She smiled sorrowfully at him before she gazed out over the river.

"I am so sorry about my father's behavior, Blade. I am so terribly sorry he tried to run you out of town, but I'm glad you stayed. I'm so glad that you defied him."

Scarlett was humiliated and extremely apologetic for Pastor Joe's dubious and un-called for behavior.

"That's all right, Scar. As far as he knows, I'm not here, I have left Carmel. Let's keep it that way. You can't tell anyone that I am still here, all right? Not anyone, Scar."

He sat down on the grass, before signaling for Scarlett to sit down beside him.

"What if he shows up at Long John Mackenzie, or sees you in town?" Scarlett became apprehensive at once.

"Don't worry about Long John, Scar, he won't give me up. Pastor Joe won't see me, I promise. Our secret is safe. You are safe. We'll be okay, Scar, you must believe me, alright?"

Blade was determined to set her mind at ease. Scarlett gazed questioningly at him, while astounded by the unexpected serenity and tranquility that had entered her heart.

"Did Pastor Joe tell you about the age-old feud between the Horaks and the Bannisters?"

"Yeah, I mean, I had no idea. It seems so silly." Scarlett was baffled by the revelation of an outrageous two-hundred-year-old feud.

"Me neither. I mean, my mom died when I was born, and my dad drank himself to death almost five years later. As far as I know, he was the last remaining Bannister, other than me."

Blade was desperate to make sense of the on-going feud between the two families that was meant to have ended decades ago.

"That's so sad for you."

Scarlett was distraught at once as Blade informed her of his parents in a shuddering and anguished voice.

"That's alright. Long John stepped in and gave me a home. I did okay." He smiled as he turned to face Scarlett.

"I mean, if I understand correctly, the feud was stupid. Over land?"

Scarlett was unable to fully comprehend the magnitude of the war between the two families.

"It was more than that, Scar. It was about power and greed. It was about Catherine Horak. Legend has it that the Horaks were responsible for the fire that devastated our land which resulted in the end of the Bannister reign and left us homeless and penniless." He became dismayed at the very suggestion that love, greed and power were responsible for altering the course of an entire family.

Scarlett lowered her head in mortification while attempting to puzzle the pieces together.

"Do you think it was my grandfather?"

Scarlett was devastated to learn that the God-fearing Horak family could very well be accountable for the Bannister's devastating losses.

"It doesn't matter, Scar. It no longer matters and carries no weight anymore. What's important is the here and now, and right now, I want to hear more about you. I just want to be with you."

"What do you want to know?" She smiled bashfully at him.

"Do you have a boyfriend?" She erupted into laughter at once.

"Really? You're asking me that? You've met Pastor Joe?" Blade smiled as he gazed into her arctic blue eyes.

"By the way, I'm really sorry that my dad treated you as offensively as he did. It was the first time a boy dared to come to my house, and I think it unsettled him." Scarlett began to explain while she noticed the sparkle in Blade's green eyes.

"Who does this barn belong to?"

Scarlett turned back to the old run-down barn that had been a fraction of Carmel for as long as she could remember.

"This is what's left of our land, Scar. Just this barn. Apparently, right here is where Catherine flung herself into the river. My dad used to tell me the story of how she held her child in her arms and jumped. Their bodies were never recovered. My grandfather's first wife. My dad used to come and sit here at night and drink himself into a stupor."

She noticed sorrow and dejection in his eyes as his voice became raucous at once.

"I'm so sorry, Blade." She whispered almost inaudibly.

He took her hands into his and held firmly onto them. "Don't be, Scar. I only wish we had met sooner or perhaps, in another time."

He spoke gently, yet the wretchedness had entirely overwhelmed him.

"I feel like we have only this moment, that we are stuck

in only one moment in time? That this is all we'll ever have? Something just feels wrong, Scar."

"Don't say that, Blade. I will meet you here every night if that's what you want, and once I turn eighteen, Pastor Joe can't keep me here against my will."

Blade Bannister had in no way at all met someone as striking and as gentle as Scarlett Rose Horak; the complete reverse of Pastor Joe.

More often than not, he bore witness to tremendous and horrendous sorrow in her eyes, while his heart reminded him of the fact that Pastor Joe possessed a compelling hold over his daughter.

He had no intimation as to why he had lingered in Carmel, but he was fraught to remain as close to Scarlett Rose as was possible. There was nothing at all to confirm to him that there could be anything more, than what they had had at that very moment.

Blade was overcome by intense sorrow as he considered all the uncertainties that were overwhelming him. He was aware of a certain fear that had engulfed him, yet he had no way to identify precisely what it was that he was fearful of. All that was around him had altered his perspective on life; a life he no longer knew how to live in.

He no longer viewed a single fraction as he once did, and he reluctantly accepted that he was different; changed and entirely altered while he had no suspicion of what to make of all the events that were taking place around him.

He was entirely new and unfamiliar with the emotions that had welled up inside of him and he dreadfully feared what they future might hold for him.

"Your mom seems sweet?" Blade was desperate to slice through the sudden silence that had beleaguered them.

"She's strict, but not as bad as my dad. Although, I must be honest, she is putty in Matthew's hands. Matthew is my older brother. My mother will never cross Pastor Joe; she will remain obedient to the Pastor until she dies!"

Scarlett became fuming once again while she was aware of an intense feeling of disappointment and resentment towards her mother.

"They're just trying to protect you, Scar. I can't say that I can blame them."

"From what?" She gazed cynically up at him.

"From guys like me."

"No Blade, my father thinks he is better than everyone else. I like you. I'm not scared of you, I want to be with you...around you." She whispered croakily.

"I like you too, Scarlett Rose, and I hope that you never fear me."

He kissed her gently while Scarlett was wholeheartedly aware of her heart that had begun to hammer ferociously. It was the first time in her entire existence that a boy had kissed her on the mouth, and it made way for feelings she had never known before.

Her body had begun to shudder as her hands were trembling frenziedly. She could smell his scent into her soul, and in no way at all, did she wish for his kiss to end.

Blade was unexpectedly intimidated by the sudden rupture of his emotions as he felt his lips against hers. The silkiness of her skin was outright enchanting while her arctic blue eyes senselessly bewitched him.

At that very instant, Blade was certain that it was a

meeting that could in no way at all, take place again. He was vulnerable in her presence and he was excruciatingly sensitive to the reality that her energy was drawing him in at a rapid speed, as though he was instantly captivated by her wholesomeness.

Blade knew at once that there could by no means at all, be a future for him that included Scarlett. They were entire worlds apart from one another; Scarlett was the wealthy Pastor's daughter while Blade was an outcast who grew up in dire poverty.

Scarlett Rose's roots were firmly planted in Carmel, while the last remaining Bannister was banished and expelled from the extraordinary village he once held a claim to. He was without any doubt that there was no possibility of any class of a future with Scarlett Rose.

"Scar, wait." He gently retreated from her while she gazed at him in utter bewilderment.

"What's the matter?" She was desperate to feel his lips on hers once again.

"We can't do this. This isn't right." He abruptly rose to his feet as he was once again nudged by the overwhelming fear that had consumed him.

"Then why did you ask me to meet you here?" She became wholly uninhabited at once.

"I don't know, Scar? I don't know what we're doing or why I am here, but all I do know is that I am here because of you."

"Then stay, Blade. Stay with me." She raised her voice while frantically terrified that he might walk away from her.

"It's late, Scarlett. You should head back home."

He placed his arms around her, and once more, he held her firmly against him. He could sense Scarlett into his soul and it unnerved him as he realized that he had no idea of how to deal adequately with the emotions that had begun to overwhelm him.

"Will you meet me tomorrow night?"

She pleaded for him to return to their surreptitious meeting venue.

"I don't know? What about on the beach?"

"My dad has grounded me. I am no longer allowed on the beach unaccompanied." The tears were once again, brimming in her eyes.

"Alright, same time tomorrow?" He replied before he

hesitantly released her hands. She hurriedly kissed him on the cheek before she turned away from him and made her way back onto the path to return home. She turned to him one more time before she waved him goodbye.

Blade stood on the cliff behind the barn for an extended period of time after she had left. He was entirely intrigued by Scarlett, yet powerless to resist her exquisiteness. Blade realized that Scarlett had no indication of how enormously her power was over him while she had no intimation of how beautiful she was.

She possessed innocence about her while her will to experience the world was slowly escaping from within. Blade grinned broadly when he realized that Pastor Joe no longer possessed the authority to shield Scarlett; her strength was determined to break down all the cages he had built to enclose her in and lock her away from the world.

While he stood watching her leave, he could in no way identify with the sudden explosion of emotions and he could even less consider why he was unable to leave Carmel when he was convincingly instructed to do so by Pastor Joe.

Blade reluctantly discovered that he was abruptly and unexpectedly thrust into a world he no longer understood.

The Weeping Prince & The Mansion in Sand

He had no experience or no knowledge of the sudden impact of all that had begun surfacing around him. Life as he knew it was over; he was utterly convinced that the journey he had reluctantly and unexpectedly begun would take him places he had never recognized before. He became terrified of all the realities as he fell to his knees and sunk his head into his hands.

He was cautiously stepping into the unfamiliar and as much as he would hesitate to take the next step; Blade felt into the innermost core of him that he could not at all retreat since the first step was taken on the night he had met Scarlett Rose.

A phenomenal war had begun brewing inside of him; he was an unwilling soldier in an unnecessary and unforeseeable war that had no possibility of an acceptable ending. Blade gazed up at the stars while he felt his entire world collapsing around him,

"I can't let her go. I don't want to." He shouted out in desperation while frantically praying that the stars would intervene before he entirely lost himself in a world he failed to make sense of.

Scarlett embraced Monday mornings which would take her away from her parents for a few hours each day for the next five mornings. Mondays were a brand-new start to a brand-new week.

She avoided her parents by any means possible and when Pastor Joe insisted on driving her to school, she was excruciatingly reminded of his relentless intimidation of her. They drove in silence while Pastor Joe glanced at her often.

It entirely demoralized him when he noticed an enormous grin on his daughter's face during the short drive to school, and when he pulled up in front of her high school, Scarlett slid out of the passenger seat without delay.

"Your mother or I will pick you up this afternoon!" He hollered out behind her, uncertain if they had perhaps, already lost Scarlett to an entire diverse world; one that Pastor Joe was certain that God would frown upon.

Scarlett hurriedly made her way over to the classroom where she met up with Alethea.

"Hey Ally!"

She swiftly placed her satchel on the ground when she reached her.

"Scarlett, hey! Why do you look so happy?"

Alethea was puzzled by the unexpected expression of

delight on Scarlett's face. In all the years that she had known Scarlett, she could barely count her joyous smiles on one hand.

"Oh nothing. I am just in a good mood."

"Okay then? Shall we go down to the beach after school?"

"I can't Ally, my parents have grounded me. Either Pastor Joe or my mom will pick me up after school, and I am in no way allowed to go to the beach unaccompanied."

Alethea stared at Scarlett in disbelief, "Why? Was it because of that outburst in Church which by the way, was awesome!"

She lifted her hand in a feeble attempt at a high five.

"Yeah, plus Pastor Joe feels you are too liberated. He thinks I am picking up bad habits from you."

Scarlett chuckled as she discovered an unforeseen expression of satisfaction on her friend's face.

"You know, my mom says it's about time that you start acting out towards your parents. I mean Scar, they totally imprison you in that house." Alethea was entirely enthusiastic to gossip while Scarlett had only Blade on her mind.

The Weeping Prince & The Mansion in Sand

"Well, at least Matthew's coming home for Christmas! Something to look forward to." Scarlett was elated that her brother would be home in less than four months.

"Yeah, your mom could never say no to him and at least most of the pressure would be off of you."

"But it's not fair, Ally. I study really hard and I get good grades. I teach Sunday school and I do all and more of what they expect from me. I have never, ever given Pastor Joe a reason not to trust me, yet they think I shamelessly run around and fraternize, as my father would say. And now ... I really like Blade...I mean, I really like him, Ally ... but Pastor Joe thinks he's left town."

"I know you're a good girl, Scar. You are such a brilliant example to the youth. I don't get it?"

"When I turn eighteen, Ally ... I am gone!"

Alethea embraced Scarlett firmly before she stepped back and gazed at Scarlett with colossal pity, "That's what my mom says, they'll never see you again."

When Blade discovered that Scarlett was altogether barred from the beach and from building her sand castles, he engaged in a heroic effort to rebuild her mansions in the sand, without her knowing.

While Scarlett was at school, he was determined to build and construct the largest sand castle that would be able to withstand any tide, any wind and any fierce storm.

He diligently spent his days on the beach while erecting the largest, most beautiful sand castle she would ever lay her eyes on. There was not much else for him to do since Pastor Joe had banished him from Carmel.

He built tirelessly and in secret and when morning approached, he would rush back and rescue what was left of his structure from the previous day. He unstintingly built each corner and each hall to perfection until he could someday; present the impeccable and glorious sand castle to her; just as she had dreamed of for almost her entire life.

He would remain on his knees while scooping and packing the sand with a plastic shovel into a bright red bucket. Afterwards, he would upend the bucket on the surface and lift it to expose the creation of a beautiful castle tower. All day long, Blade would spoon out the moat and pack the walls. He would rummage for bottle tops that would be used for sentries while Popsicle sticks would act as bridges, but a sand castle, one worthy of Scarlett Rose, would be carefully and meticulously built.

As the tide grew higher each day and as they came closer each evening, he could almost hear the ocean savagely reprimand him, "These are my castles!"

Blade would jump to his feet while he felt no sorrow or any regret. He anticipated the reality that the sea would collect that which belonged to it and while witnessing an enormous wave crash into Scarlett's castle which was sucked back into the sea, Blade smiled desolately.

Scarlett would find it utterly daunting to witness the devastation of her castles while she would almost certainly hover frantically over them in an attempt to guard them. Blade was determined to someday, find a method to block the crashing waves from seeping through the walls of Scarlett's mansions in the sand and preserve them for her, for all eternity.

# CARTER JETHRO

Barely a month after Scarlett's astonishing outburst in Pastor Joe's Church, he and Lily called for an urgent family meeting after dinner one cold, winter's evening. Scarlett had habitually met Blade out at the barn almost each night, and it seemed to her as though she could tolerate her father's cruelty and her mother's obedience to Pastor Joe with greater ease although not entirely effortlessly.

She had avoided run-ins with Pastor Joe at every corner and kept herself cooped up in her bedroom with each opportunity that presented itself to her. She fervently and sincerely apologized to the congregation in Church one Sunday morning just as the sermon was about to begin, although she in no way at all, regretted her outlandish behavior.

"I know. I know there is something out there for me. I have to try, I have to find it." She whispered as she gazed out through her window and stared up at the stars.

When Scarlett reached the dining room, Lily and Pastor Joe had only recently taken their seats around the dining room table. She slid into an empty seat directly across from her mother and folded her hands in an attempt to appear courageous, even though her heart was hammering ferociously in her chest.

"Scarlett Rose. Your mother and I have spoken. You will turn eighteen early next year and we have decided to free you up a little. We want to give you a little more freedom and somewhat more privileges."

Lily smiled as she gazed over at Scarlett. Scarlett, in turn, glowered at hearing her father's rapid and unexpected change of heart. She remained silent, uncertain of what Pastor Joe was saying to her, but cautious of his unexpected emancipation of her.

"What your father is saying, Scar is that we have decided to allow you out to the library or to the milkshake parlor once in a while."

Scarlett smiled nervously as she guardedly turned back to Pastor Joe. "Really? Why?" She glared at her father in utter disbelief.

"Yes, Scarlett Rose. As long as your responsibilities towards the Church are not neglected or compromised and as long as your school work does not suffer. I think that you are growing up and that it's important to mingle with people your age. I trust you, Scarlett Rose."

"Wow, thank you father." Scarlett was elated at once as she jumped from her seat.

"There is one condition, however ..." Pastor Joe turned to Lily before he turned back to Scarlett.

"You will be accompanied by Carter Jethro at all times. This is not open for discussion, Scarlett and there will be no negotiation on this matter. These are my terms. I have thought long and hard about this matter, and I have made up my mind."

Scarlett was horrified by her father's unreasonable demands once again. "No!" She retaliated at once.

"I don't want to go out with Carter! I don't need a chaperone, Pastor Joe! You just said that you trusted me?"

"He is an outstanding member of the community and comes from an upstanding and highly regarded family. We have spoken to the Jethros and they are fairly keen for this union."

"Union? What union? What are you talking about?" Scarlett became panicky at once.

"We feel, your mother and I feel that the two of you are

better suited as a couple in the long run."

"What long run? I don't understand? You are choosing a suitor for me? Like ... a husband?"

Scarlett yelled through her tears that had begun to roll intensely down her cheeks. "I won't do it, father! I hardly know Carter!"

"He will be a fine choice, Scarlett Rose. He is well-bred and well-respected, and he is my choice for you."

"You don't get to decide or choose what or who I want, Pastor Joe! You can't tell me who to love and who to spend the rest of my life with! I am not even eighteen yet, and you want to marry me off? What about college?"

"If you willingly choose to obey me, Scarlett and should you disobey the laws of the Church, I will have no other option than to send you away to a convent until you turn twenty-one. You will in no way attend college or university. I will shun you and banish you from Carmel forever. You will be dead to me."

Pastor Joe had remained composed, yet he was determined that Scarlett entirely comprehend the severity of the wrath that he would unleash upon her.

"In that case, Pastor Joe, I elect to remain grounded. I am already dead to you! You don't give a shit about me or how I feel! Mother?" Scarlett abruptly rose to her feet once again while her tears had continued to flow unreservedly from her eyes. Lily bowed her head while Pastor Joe glared firmly at Scarlett.

"Mind your language! Oh no, Scarlett. There are no choices. I am not asking you, this isn't simply a request; I am ordering you. Carter Jethro has been invited for dinner tonight and you will be on your very best behavior. Should you defy me, I would have no other choice than to send you away."

"I hate you! This is bullshit! You and mama are bullshit!" Scarlett pounced with her fists onto the dining room table before she turned her back on Pastor Joe and rushed back upstairs.

Scarlett was horrified at the mere deliberation of dating Carter Jethro, a boy she barely knew but saw often at Church. They had grown up together but were no longer and by no means on friendly terms. Scarlett had persistently snubbed him, yet other than the casual hellos and goodbyes at Church, they had nothing much to say to one another.

She could barely envision herself and Carter as a couple, let alone spend the rest of her life with him. Carter was a devoted book lover and a committed worshipper of Pastor Joe and his

Church. Although he was in no way awkward looking, the mere fact that his family was so entirely intertwined with the Horaks, discouraged her at once.

When Carter Jethro arrived promptly at eight o' clock for dinner, Scarlett had dressed herself in a warm outfit that had entirely covered her up. She was anxious for the night to be over; she was desperate to return to Blade who was waiting for her at the barn.

"Good evening, sir."

She heard Carter's voice as she hurriedly laid the dining room table.

"Good evening, son." Pastor Joe shook his hand and led him into the dining room. Carter carried in a bunch of flowers and instantly handed them to Lily.

"Thank you for inviting me, Ma'am."

"You're welcome, Carter. Please take a seat."

"Hello, Scarlett." He smiled broadly at her before he took his seat at the dining room table.

"Hi." Scarlett sighed as she sat down on the empty seat directly across from him. Once dinner was served, Pastor Joe turned to Carter.

"Carter, your father tells me that you will join him at Jethro-Horak in the new year?"

"Oh, yes sir."

"Will you be directly involved in the development and erection of shopping complexes?"

"Oh, no sir. I am too boring. I will be handling all the financials for the firm. Father has enrolled me in an accounting course … that's more my thing."

"Oh, I see. Smart boy."

"Scarlett, what are your plans for the new year?" Carter was eager to learn more about her ideals for the future.

"Apparently, I will be getting married and popping out babies." She replied without lifting her head from her dinner plate.

"Oh my." Carter was absolutely confused by her unexpected irritation.

"Scarlett Rose!" Lily remarked in horror.

"Pay no attention to her, Carter." Pastor Joe turned to

Scarlett and glared angrily at her. They sat in silence while enjoying the rest of their meal. Scarlett had lost her appetite from the moment that Carter had walked in while she could barely take her mind off of Blade who she was certain, was waiting for her.

As soon as dinner was over, Pastor Joe and Carter made their way into the living room while Scarlett assisted Lily with clearing the dining room table.

"Ma'am, you have to speak to Pastor Joe, I can't do this! I don't want to." She begged her mother to urge her father to reconsider his irrational and superfluous demands.

"Scarlett Rose, he doesn't listen to me, you know that?" Lily was conquered by the abrupt compassion she instantly felt for her daughter.

"Just be patient and go along with his rules. You'll see, everything will sort itself out. I promise you, all will sort itself out." Lily placed a loving arm on Scarlett's shoulder.

"Scarlett Rose!"

Pastor Joe called frenetically out to Scarlett who smiled despondently at her mother. She hurriedly made her way into the living room where he was seated with Carter Jethro across from him; in the exact same seat that Blade sat at on the night Pastor Joe sent him away.

"Carter is leaving. Will you walk him out?"

"Sure."

Scarlett sighed as Carter got up and firmly shook Pastor Joe's hand. As they reached the front door, Carter turned abruptly,

"Goodbye Mrs. Horak!" He shouted out in his usual cheerful and pleasant manner. When they reached the front porch, Carter turned to Scarlett.

"Walk with me to the gate, please?"

Scarlett followed him as he led her out to the gate. He had just opened the gate to walk through when he suddenly turned back to Scarlett,

"Listen Scar. I know your father's hard on you, but it's simply because he loves you. This thing that he wants between us, will never work. It's never going to happen; you and I both know that. I know that for a fact, but we could help one another out if you're interested? This thing, this pretense could benefit us both."

"How? What do you mean?" Scarlett was suddenly confused.

"Let's just go along with it. Nothing will ever come of it, Scar and I have zero expectations of anything happening, but at least, you get to come out of the house every so often."

"Why Carter? Why would you do this for me?"

She was once again puzzled by his odd behavior, yet she liked him a little more than she did when he had arrived for dinner.

"I have my own secrets, Scarlett."

"Like what? You're such a goody two shoes! You are just about perfect." She giggled in her sleeve at the mere thought of Carter Jethro carrying around secrets.

"I'm by no means perfect, far from actually. Scarlett, you cannot tell anyone. Promise? You must swear it."

"I promise, Carter, what could be so bad?" She chuckled once again, relieved that Carter too, was entirely in opposition of their proposed union.

"I, I don't, I don't really like girls. Not like that, you know?" He became bashful and utterly embarrassed at once.

Scarlett gasped for air when she realized what Carter was telling her.

"You're kidding! You're gay? I mean, you're gay?" She whispered in a desperate attempt to shield his secret from her father. Carter hung his head in dishonor as he instantly questioned whether his confession would remain a secret. Scarlett rubbed his arm and felt pity for him at once.

"Your secret is safe with me, Carter, I swear, nobody will ever find out. Not from me, anyways."

"So, you see, Scar. We'll be helping one another. You get to leave the house and hopefully meet someone spectacular while I get to see Jonas on the side ... in secret. We can both benefit from the pretense. I am just not ready to tell the world yet. Pastor Joe, you know?"

Scarlett smiled and instantaneously agreed to his proposal. "Yeah, I know. Pastor Joe would be determined to send you away in search of a cure. I think we have a deal, Carter Jethro." She flung her arms around him, and firmly embraced him.

Pastor Joe was peering cautiously through the living room window in an attempt to observe Scarlett's demeanor around Carter Jethro. He smiled when he noticed Scarlett's sudden and unexpected smile and he sighed with relief when he witnessed her embrace him with poise. When Lily entered the living room, he immediately released the curtain and disgracefully stepped back.

"I think she'll be alright, Lily. It seems as though she likes him."

Lily shook her head before she gathered the dirty dishes and returned to the kitchen. "You shouldn't be spying on our daughter like that, Joseph."

Lily found his spying on Scarlett utterly distasteful and once again questioned why she had been so blind to Pastor Joe for all the years.

To Scarlett's utter surprise, she and Carter had become firm friends almost straight away. Pastor Joe was adamant that she refrains from returning to the beach as she was to spend all her free time studying for her final year at school.

He would on occasion allow her out to the movies with Carter solely when a gospel film was being screened, but he was obstinate that she adheres to her curfew. Carter was effortlessly able to convince Pastor Joe to permit Scarlett to enjoy a milkshake with him once in a while.

He regularly met up with Jonas at the movies or at the milkshake parlor and the three unlikely souls became firm friends in an extremely short while. Scarlett was anxious to keep Carter's secret while Carter was desperate for Scarlett to meet a boy that would be more suited for her.

"Scar, why don't you invite a boy to come with us? Surely there must be someone you have a crush on?"

"No, I don't Carter. I'm just grateful to get out of the house. I like spending time with you and Jonas."

Carter would snugly embrace her, and he silently wished that she would soon meet "the one who loves her soul" as he would habitually refer to Jonas.

# SECRETS

When October had made its unexpected appearance, Blade and Scarlett had met one another almost as if on schedule night after night, behind the old barn on the cliff as they had numerous nights before.

Although the nights were growing colder and damper, there was no gust of wind or a rain storm severe enough that could keep Scarlett away from any one of her reunions with Blade.

They would sit behind the barn while overlooking the river as Scarlett would dream of the promising future that she had planned with Blade. She would spend hours planning and mapping out the day that she would turn eighteen, and she grew increasingly anxious for that very day to show up.

She had informed Blade early on about her agreement with Carter Jethro, and after his initial hesitation, he was thankful that she was given the opportunity to leave the solitude of her bedroom and her home.

"I can't wait for us to leave Carmel, Blade." She held firmly onto him while counting the days down to her graduation.

"I turn eighteen early next year, and then we can leave together and never come back here. Just you and I, forever. We can go far away, and never come back...just you and I. There will be no Pastor Joe to keep us apart ever again!" She swore during one of their nightly meetings.

"Scar, don't think that far ahead. Let's just live one day at a time, for now. You've got your whole life ahead of you, and you might just meet someone new. You might feel differently, things change so fast." Blade was at once terrified of the reality of losing Scarlett Rose even though he had a nudging feeling that she was never his.

"I don't want anyone else, Blade. I want you. I, I love you. I want to be with you. I want to make plans with you. I want this, ou and me." She gazed at him forlornly as her tears flowed enthusiastically down her cheeks.

"I am not who's right for you, Scar. You know that? Your father is right ..." He was agonizingly aware of the differences between their families.

"I am a poor boy from the wrong side of the tracks. You

deserve wonderful, Scar. A magnificent life. A beautiful tomorrow with someone that will stick around." He was devastated by the authenticity that he could in no way ever, be the man by Scarlett Rose's side.

"You're a poor boy because of my family, Blade. I love you! You are my wonderful life! I choose you, Blade! You are all that keeps me going, you are all that I want...don't take that away from me. I am begging you, Blade...don't leave me here! Wait for me, please." She shouted through her tears in a desperate attempt to convince Blade that her entire world would collapse without him.

"Pastor Joe is just a man, he isn't God. He is just a man! Don't let him do this to us, Blade!"

He pulled her closer to him and held her firmly in his arms. "I love you, Scar, so much. But ..."

She interrupted him at once. "But nothing, Blade. But nothing. Just wait for me! I am begging you Blade, wait for me. Don't leave me here without you. I don't care about anything if you aren't a part of it. My heart won't let you go. Shit, this hurts."

Scarlett desperately pleaded for him to linger and wait for her. "Please say you'll wait for me. I'll grow up soon, Blade.

I'm saving myself just for you, don't give up on me. Don't give up on us. Please, Blade." She whispered through the restricting lump in her throat.

"I am here for you, Scar, only because of you, but I, me, this is not enough. You, you just don't understand, Scar and I don't know how to tell you." He whispered as she clung firmly to him.

"I don't want to understand, Blade. I don't want to hear any of this! Just tell me one thing, do you love me?" She retreated while she gazed firmly into his eyes. Blade stared at her before he took her face into her hands,

"Scar, more than anything, I love you. I love, love you. I have never felt this way before, and I don't understand why all of this is happening, and you don't either. This isn't what is real, none of this is."

He paused to take in a deep breath before Scarlett interrupted him once more, "This is real. All of this, it's happening because you found me and this is how it should be. Please Blade, please, just wait for me. I don't want to live without you. Nothing you say will change how I feel, nothing."

Scar erupted into tears as Blade held her firmly against

him once again. He was painfully aware of the tears that were shimmering in his eyes while he knew that somehow, their beautiful story was bound to end in tragedy.

"Scarlett Rose, we can't keep doing this. Things are not as they seem. There are things that you don't know, or understand about me. I don't even understand it. I just know that I am here because of you, and I don't know how to let go? I don't know what the next step is?"

"Blade, only for a little while longer, I promise. Please wait for me. You are home to me."

At home and at Church, Pastor Joe and Lily became increasingly contented with Scarlett's improved behavior.

She seemed gradually increasingly comfortable with her restrictions and no longer implored her parents to allow her out onto the beach or to visit with Alethea. She would regularly gush about Carter to Lily, and she no longer confronted Pastor Joe about his domination of her.

She willingly attended each Church service as was expected of her, and she no longer intentionally fought against her parents or the Scripture.

Lily grew progressively distraught as she noticed the

downright wretchedness in Scarlett's eyes and realized with a startle that her daughter was putting up a front to keep the tranquility in the family.

She was certain that Pastor Joe had crushed her spirit and that their daughter was fading away right in front of them.

When Lily attempted to discuss her concerns with Pastor Joe, he shrugged it off by implying that the Holy Spirit had merely returned to their daughter.

After dinner one evening, Lily knocked gently on her daughter's bedroom door as soon as Pastor Joe had left for his weekly rounds at the Carmel Children's Hospital. "Come in?"

Scarlett sat on her bed while studying for an upcoming test.

"Scarlett Rose?" Her mother hesitantly made her way into Scarlett's bedroom.

"Ma'am, is something the matter?" Scarlett became ill at ease at once. Never before did her mother make a deliberate point of entering her daughter's bedroom other than when she was nursing her for a common cold or the flu.

"Please don't call me that, Scar. I am your mother.

Address me as your mama."

By the expression on Lily's face, Scarlett became anxious at once. "I, I don't understand? What's the matter? Did something happen?"

"Scarlett Rose, just mama is fine." Lily sat down beside her before she took the handbook from Scarlett's hands and placed it on the bed beside her.

"I've made some mistakes, Scar. I've let him destroy you, your spirit. I've stood by and watched him do that. I was the good wife, but I am a terrible mother."

Scarlett was at once aware of her mother's tears that were brimming in her eyes. "What do you mean, mama?"

Scarlett nervously dabbed at the tears that had rolled onto her mother's cheek.

"He's too hard on you. You should be young. You should be free. He keeps you far too caged. He shouldn't have the power to force Carter Jethro onto you like that. You should be free to love a man of your choosing, Scar. It's all right to have fun. It's all right to be careless and reckless once in a while. I feel like, I feel like we've lost you?"

# The Weeping Prince & The Mansion in Sand

Lily had begun to sob violently as Scarlett placed her arms firmly around her mother.

"It's alright, mother. I like Carter. At least he gets me out of the house." Scarlett was altogether caught off guard by her mother's sudden and unexpected behavior.

"It's not alright, baby. God doesn't want this for you. God doesn't work like this, my precious Scar. I see how you look at Carter, you are good friends, but nothing more. I want it all for you, Scar and if you want to be with that Bannister boy, if he makes you happy, then I can live with that. Love Scar, is what this life is all about. He frightens your father. Your father carries many secrets, my dear Scar and Blade Bannister frightens him. He comes from a good family. Their only mistake was that they were beaten down by the Horaks. Love is everything, Scarlett Rose. They were once an upstanding family. They were wealthy and a force to be reckoned with. The Horaks were cruel and heartless, and because of them, because of all their dishonesty, the Bannisters lost everything."

"Then why don't you stand up to him, mama? Why do you let him treat you the way he does, us?" Scarlett questioningly probed her mother at once. Lily bowed her head in utter disgrace before she turned back to Scarlett.

"I let it go on for too long. I thought I was being a good wife and mother, but I am a terrible mother. Matthew couldn't wait to leave once he had graduated, and you'll be next. Your father will never change, Scarlett Rose. It's too late."

Her mother sobbed fiercely once again as Scarlett held her firmly against her.

"He thinks he's being a good father, mama. Let him be. I'm tired of fighting him. Just let him be. But mama, you need to find a way to be happy. You cannot let him treat you like this."

Lily gazed back at Scarlett and noticed a lost tear that had rolled down her cheek.

By the look in Scarlett's eyes, Lily was convinced that Scarlett had given up and surrendered to Pastor Joe's will. She had given up on all that was significant to her, and for just an instant, Lily was certain that her daughter was dying inside.

Scarlett had grown tremendously delicate while her long hair flowed unkempt down her back. The sparkle that once was evident for all to see had made way for an expression of defeat.

"You are so unhappy, my girl. It's as though you walk around by design. You have no voice; you have no freedom and you have no life."

The Weeping Prince & The Mansion in Sand

Scarlett was certain that her mother's heart had shattered into a million fractions.

"It'll be alright, mama. I'll be okay, you'll see." Scarlett whispered above a confining lump in her throat.

Lily rose to her feet and embraced her daughter one more time, "I love you, Scar. Don't you ever lose that fighting spirit of yours. It scares your father, it makes him nervous."

"I love you too, mama. Thank you, thank you, mama." She smiled through her sudden rupture of tears.

As Lily turned to walk out, Scarlett realized how utterly broken and overpowered her mother was. She was devastatingly distressed to witness her mother in such a demoralizing manner, and she was enraged at Pastor Joe once more.

Not only had Pastor Joe destroyed all that was sacred to her, but he destroyed her mother's sense of worth a long time ago. Lily was exhausted; a man like Pastor Joe was demanding and challenging at the best of times. For a moment, Scarlett wondered if her mother had perhaps given up, just as she almost had.

As Lily closed Scarlett's bedroom door behind her, she was instantly startled to find Blade standing outside of her bedroom window.

"Get in here! Before someone sees you!" Scarlett frantically opened her bedroom window for Blade to climb through. He firmly placed his arms around her waist, and pulled her firmly against him,

"Ooooh I missed you, Scarlett Rose." She placed her index finger against his lips,

"Sshh, I missed you too, handsome." He kissed her gently before he collapsed onto her bed.

Scarlett slid in beside him, elated that Blade had snuck in to see her. "Why are your hands covered in sea sand? Were you on the beach?"

She frantically attempted to wipe the sand from his hands.

"Yes, I walked along the beach so that nobody could see me. Tonight, feels like it's so far away and I couldn't wait until then to see you. Do you have plans with that Carter dude today?"

He lied about the sand on his hands, but he was desperate to keep the secret of building the sand castle for Scarlett for just a while longer.

"No, not today, but I'm glad you're here. I miss you more and more each day." Scarlett kissed him firmly on the lips.

"Yeah, yeah. You just want to kiss me!" He teased before he forcefully kissed her. She burst out into laughter before Blade hurriedly attempted to silence her.

As though in one motion, her bedroom door swung open as Pastor Joe appeared in her doorway in all his supposed brilliance. "Scarlett Rose! Who are you talking to?"

He demanded at once before he made his way into her bedroom. Scarlett hurriedly glanced around her, and to her utter astonishment, Blade was nowhere to be seen. The window had been shut and the curtains were drawn. "No-one father, I was, here's no-one." She whispered, deathly afraid that he might uncover the fact that Blade was hiding somewhere in her bedroom.

"I heard you Scar. Laughing and giggling!" He was enraged as he peeked in under her bed, and rummaged through her closet.

"Pastor Joe! Stop! Here is no-one here! I was studying out loud and was giggling at my silly voice. Here is no-one here!" She yelled out in desperation before Pastor Joe glanced around one more time.

Pastor Joe mumbled incoherently under his breath before he turned to leave while he was certain that his paranoia was overshadowing him. As he shut her door, Scarlett at once sighed with immense relief. She turned to the window and discovered Blade standing there once more.

"Wow! That was real quick! Where did you go? It's like you just vanished?" She giggled softly as he made his way back to her.

"You must have done this so many times before! You are a pro!" She poked accusingly at him.

"Actually, never before." He lay down beside her as he held her protectively in his arms.

"I don't know what's happening here, Scar but it scares me."

Scarlett was at once sensitive to his instant anguish. "Don't let it frighten you, Blade. I love you. I want to spend the rest of my life with you. Don't let Pastor Joe jolt you like this."

Scarlett was desperate for Blade to understand that she had no life without him.

"It's going to end, Scarlett. One way or another, it'll end, someday, I know it."

"Don't say that! Don't you ever say that again, Blade Bannister. I won't let it! Do you understand? I won't let it!" She was frantic while she was engulfed in terror almost at once. He held her firmly in his arms before she drifted off to sleep.

The following morning, while Scarlett was staring at her exam paper, her mind drifted off to Blade once more. She was reminded by the age-old family feud that seemed to be the awful reason that kept Scarlett and Blade apart.

As soon as she had completed her test, Scarlett hurriedly made her way into the library, hoping to learn more about Carmel's history and the truth regarding the Horak and Bannister families. She had barely entered the library when she unexpectedly ran into Carter and Jonas, who were just on their way out.

"Hey Scar!" Carter swiftly kissed her on her cheek while Jonas hurriedly embraced her.

"Hello, you two handsome boys!" She was in high spirits to run into the pair.

"Are you going in? Do you want us to come with you?"

"No, that's all right, Jonas. I was just hoping to do research, but nothing important."

"Alright then, we're going over to Mindy's if you need us." Carter gently squeezed her arm.

"If Pastor Joe asks, remember I was here with you!"

Scarlett reminded Carter of their on-going deception.

There was an eerie silence in the library that seemed deserted and almost forgotten. Scarlett adored reading, but she was compelled to read only the books that were prescribed to her by Pastor Joe.

She would regularly sneak into the library when she had a break in between classes where she would sit quietly in a corner and indulge in a Wilbur Smith mystery or a Danielle Steel novel.

Scarlett was saddened by the reality that the majority of the youth had access to the libraries through the mere touch or command on a smart phone. Books were read on the screens of computers and tablets, and the authenticity of a book seemed lost to the world forever. Scarlett adored the smell of a book, and she cherished the feel of the turn of the pages by her hand.

Scarlett was at once relieved that the library was abandoned; it was entirely out of the ordinary for any student to do research in the library while they were all equipped with access to the internet at home; something her father refused her access to.

She was desperate to learn more about the Bannister/Horak feud and anxiously made her way to the historical subdivision of the library. She had instantaneously found the book to Carmel's history and when she turned to take a seat at a study desk, she spotted Blade in the passageway ahead of her.

Her stomach turned, and her heart began to thump when she saw him standing there. His trademark black leather jacket hung snugly around him, and his torn jeans completed his appeal.

She loved surveilling the silhouette of the man she utterly and unreservedly adored. Scarlett smiled when she saw him watching her, and hurriedly made her way over to him.

"You pop up everywhere these days!" She flung her arms around him and gently kissed him.

"I just miss you, Scar."

She at once noticed the sea sand on his hands yet again. "You were on the beach again, right? Long John Mackenzie is going to fire you!" She giggled as she again attempted to swab the sand from his hands.

"Don't tell him." Blade giggled while he held her firmly against him.

"What are you doing here?"

"I, I was looking for a book on the history of Carmel. You know, to learn more about the feud."

She was anxious to observe Blade's response.

"Oh Scarlett, let it go. I am the last Bannister, and it's no longer important to me. It really never was."

He was desperate to keep Scarlett from delving into the truth about the devastating fire on their land.

"It's important to me, Blade. I want to try and set things right. If the Horaks were responsible for costing your family your land, the world should know. Your reputation should be restored. My mom says that your family were upstanding members of the community and that the Horaks were responsible for your downfall, I want the world to know, Blade."

"Scar, listen to me. There's nothing to set right. There's no point. I don't care what anyone thinks they know about me or my family. What's done has been done." He began to explain before he became silent.

"What do you mean, there's no point? There's always a point, Blade. The truth must come out. Your family lost everything because of mine. You've been banished and condemned because Pastor Joe is afraid that the truth might come out. I know my father, Blade. You scare him, and because of that, we will always be together like this. We are always going to hide." She became anxious at once.

"There is no point, Scar, just let it go. Promise me, you'll let it go. I don't want justice. I just want peace. This feud will only ever end when either the last Bannister or the last Horak dies. It will die with me, Scar, let it."

He was beseeching her while it left Scarlett feeling unnerved straight away. "Promise me, Scar!"

He placed both his hands on her shoulders and gazed at her in utter revulsion.

"It won't die with you. Our children will be Bannisters, they will be proudly known as Bannisters. I will become a Bannister someday, and I will be proud of the name. It's not fair. You make it sound as though, almost as though it's going to be over soon? Like, are you saying that Pastor Joe will out-live you? Are you saying that I will never carry your name, or have your children?" She whispered hoarsely through the sudden fear that had engulfed her entire core.

"No Scarlett. That's not what I'm saying, it's just, I am the last Bannister to be caught up in this. It will end with me. It has to end with me."

Scarlett grabbed his hands into hers as her tears lay shallow in her eyes, "What about our children? I won't let it end with you! There was once a Horak and Bannister union, and there will be again! And I would be honored to be the mother of our children, Bannister children! I want to set things right for you, for us and for our children someday. What are you saying, Blade? You're scaring me!"

"Oh Scar ..."

"Miss Horak, did you find what you're looking for?" The librarian, Mrs. Hughes had appeared behind Scarlett almost out of the blue. She became anxious at once while desperately afraid that Mrs. Hughes would gossip to the town's folk about seeing her in the library in Blade's company.

"I did yes, thank you Ma'am." Scarlett turned around at once to discover that Blade had once again disappeared almost right in front of her.

"Alright, we'll be closing in an hour."

"Thank you, I am done anyway." She smiled warmly at Mrs. Hughes before she hurriedly walked out of the library.

"Where have you been, Scarlett Rose?" Pastor Joe was enraged when Scarlett returned home from her brief visit to the library.

"I, I was at the library, father. You can check with Mrs. Hughes." Once again, Scarlett Rose detected extreme anger and resentment in her father's voice.

"Joseph Horak! Enough! I gave Scarlett permission to visit the library. How do you expect her to complete any of her projects without the internet?" Lily had become livid as she directly opposed Pastor Joe.

"What project?" He turned to Lily at once.

Scarlett stepped in between her parents and unswervingly, yet fearlessly, she faced her father head on.

"History, father. It's a history project." She was determined to stand up to her father and defend Lily at all cost.

"Of what?" He was adamant to catch Scarlett out in a lie.

"About local feuds in the history of Carmel." She lied but at the same time, she was desperate to analyze the expression on his face. Pastor Joe became ashen at once.

"What feuds? Who have you been talking to, Scarlett?"

He grabbed at her arm while his anger had enthusiastically escalated.

"Joseph! Let go of her! Why are you so paranoid?" Lily bellowed before she grabbed his hand, releasing Pastor Joe's grip on his daughter.

"Is there something I should know, Pastor Joe?" Scarlett was daring yet determined to corner her father into the truth.

"What are you talking about, Scar?" Lily turned to face Scarlett.

"Ask him, mama. Ask him about a fire that devastated the Bannister lands and left them homeless and penniless. As him about the deal he made with the devil himself and then mama, ask him where his wealth comes from? How he stole the Bannister land when the Horaks set fire to their lands. Ask him, mama!" She replied almost hysterically before she made her way into the house and up to her bedroom.

"What is she talking about, Joseph?" Lily was utterly confused by Scarlett's unexpected implication.

"I think, I think she's found out about the Bannister/Horak feud and she must suspect that we were responsible for the fire, which of course, is a complete lie. I am going to find out who she's been talking to." Pastor Joe was unnerved and anxious at once. "And who does she think she is? Calling you mama?"

"I *am* her mama, Joseph. She is not a soldier, she is my daughter and she will address me as mama."

"You are becoming too soft, Lily. And those bizarre accusations?"

"Doesn't the Dear Lord reveal the truth at all times?" Lily turned away from Pastor Joe and made her way back into the kitchen.

On the final day of school, the last day that Scarlett would ever walk through the gates of her high school, she felt an abrupt sense of reprieve now that her school career had finally come to an end. The graduation ceremony was scheduled for the following day while Scarlett had no intention of sitting through the entire circus. As she made her way to her classroom, she found Alethea anxiously waiting for her.

"Scar! Did you hear? You are valedictorian!" Alethea excitedly embraced her. Scarlett sighed almost at once. It was a position she had expected but lacked any desire to fulfill.

"You should be proud, Scar!" Alethea was puzzled by her

unwillingness to participate.

"It's just because I am Pastor Joe's daughter, Ally."

"Well, just see that you prepare a brilliant speech, all right?" Alethea patted her on the back before she turned away from her.

Scarlett awoke early on the morning of her graduation from high school and despondently made her way over to her bedroom window. As she gazed out through her bedroom window, she noticed a young couple jogging in the park right across from their home.

She smiled when she witnessed the obvious bliss between them, and she secretly yearned for an authentic and liberal life with the man that she had adored. She was at once jolted back into reality when there was a soft knock on her bedroom door, "Come in!" She turned to make her way over to her closet.

"Scarlett Rose?" Lily stepped in before she hurriedly closed the door behind her.

"Mama, what's the matter?" Scarlett was at once startled to witness the wretchedness in her mother's eyes.

"Sit down, Scar, please?" Lily made her way to the edge of Scarlett's bed and slowly sat down while she signaled for her daughter to sit down beside her. Scarlett noticed an envelope in her mother's hand while fear had begun to make its way into Scarlett's heart.

When Scarlett nervously sat down beside her mother, Lily handed her the envelope, "Scar, you've been such a good daughter. You've worked so hard to get through this final phase of your childhood. Soon, you'll be all grown up and ready to take on the world, just as you should."

Lily paused to take in a deep breath. "I want you to leave this town in the New Year, after Christmas. I've saved over the years without Pastor Joe knowing. I want you to take this and go. I want you to dream many dreams, Scar and I want you to follow them all. Go and be wonderful and find your place in the world. Find that which makes you happy. Go out, and be wonderful, Scar...you don't belong here. You don't belong under Pastor Joe. Get far away from here and from him, my precious Scarlett. Follow your heart and do whatever it takes to be happy and free. You are a prisoner here and I don't want this life for you. I want more, I want better for you. Go find Blade. Take him with you. Have life, Scar."

Lily's tears were shimmering in her eyes as she realized that the time had come to finally release her daughter. "But please, please just be here for one last Christmas. I am asking for you and Matthew to be under the same roof, just one more time. And then you run, Scar, you run as fast as your legs can carry you."

"Mama?" Scarlett could barely make sense of what her

mother was saying.

"Don't marry that boy Carter Jethro, Scar. Marry whomever you want. Be free. Be young, that's all I ask of you. Be happy. And love. Love the one you want."

Scarlett embraced her mother and held her firmly against her while her own tears were bucketing from her eyes. "I love you, mama. What will you do? I can't leave you here alone with Pastor Joe?"

"Listen to me child, I will take care of Pastor Joe. You, you must go. I will be just fine. Once in a while, send me a postcard and just let me know that you are all right. I will miss you so much Scarlett, but I love you too much to sit here and watch you die slowly. I love you, my precious Scarlett Rose."

"Oh mama! I love you too! Thank you, mama."

"Enough now, you are to tell not a soul about this, alright? Now, get ready, the ceremony will start in less than an hour!"

As her mother walked out of Scarlett's bedroom, she hurriedly opened up the envelope. Inside she found a cashier's check that left Scarlett staggered. Her mother had saved enough money for tuition at any university her heart had desired with a sufficient amount left to subsist for years after.

Scarlett pressed the envelope firmly against her while joy and relief had entirely overwhelmed her. She was to be free soon; she was free to escape with Blade to a place that her soul longs for, where Pastor Joe could never find her.

For the first time in her life, she had a tomorrow to look forward to.

She could make plans and tailor-make her life into any world she desired. She was no longer compelled to bow down to any of Pastor Joe's set of laws and she could freely worship her God in the way she was nudged to, since she was only a little girl.

In less than two months, Scarlett Rose would no longer be subjected to his wrath or the fear that he had instilled in her over the years. As she mulled over all that was waiting for her, Scarlett felt immense excitement and anticipation well up inside of her.

When Scarlett reached the soccer field of her high school, she was thrilled to notice that all the graduates had diligently taken their seats. Her parents had found seats in one of the family member rows, while Scarlett scurried to find Alethea. She hurriedly slid in beside her friend and grabbed her hand in anticipation of their graduation,

"Ally! Today is the day!"

"I know, right!"

They both giggled at one another's enthusiasm.

Mr. Myers made his way to the podium before he hurriedly turned to face the graduates, "Today, is an extraordinary day for all of our graduates. Not only does it signify the end of a long twelve-year history with our school, but today marks the beginning of their adulthood and the start of their beautiful futures. Some of you will embark on careers, other will attend college or universities while some will get married and become homemakers. Whatever you do, remember to always do it with the same pride you concluded your last year of school with. Scarlett Rose, would you say a few words, please?"

Scarlett took in a deep breath when she stood up. She straightened her graduation gown and slowly made her way up to the podium. When she turned to face her fellow classmates, she became nervous at once.

She glanced around over the crowd that were quietly seated, and at once noticed Blade standing silently in the distance. She smiled broadly before she turned back to the graduates,

"I think that Mr. Myers covered it all in his speech, but what I would like to say is that we should be proud. We've worked extremely hard and we gave back to the community of Carmel. We are good boys and girls and we gave it our all. I would like to thank Mr. Myers for being an outstanding Headmaster. To all the teachers that have taught us and led us throughout the years; we graciously thank you for your exceptional patience and extremely hard work. To our parents; thank you for guiding us and teaching us of values and morals. We thank you for the discipline that was instilled in us, and we ask you to guide us and lead us as we embark upon our newest journeys. To my mother, Lily Horak; thank you mama. Thank you for the courage you have taught me to own. Thank you for your unconditional love and support. Thank you, mama, for believing in me and for having faith in me. Thank you for loving me mama, more than you love yourself. I love you, mama."

When she stepped down, Lily smiled as she looked on in pride at her daughter. Pastor Joe was disappointed that she failed to recognize him in her upbringing and in no way mentioned him in her speech.

For an instant, a twinge of sadness made its way into his

heart which lodged into the innermost core of him. Scarlett hastily glanced around and was at once saddened that Blade had disappeared as though he was not there at all.

# THE SANDCASTLE

December approached far too gradually and leisurely for Scarlett. Ever since the day that her mother had presented her what she would regularly refer to as the "ultimate gift", Scarlett could barely linger patiently in anticipation of December showing up while hoping that it would leave just as speedily as it had was supposed to have arrived.

Throughout October and November, she had devotedly met up with Blade at the barn on the cliff night after night. They had spent their nights under the stars declaring their commitment to each other while falling deeper in love with one another. She had excitedly informed Blade of her mother's selfless gift which had carried her blessing along with it and she swore to Blade that his wait would almost be over.

Blade was unexpectedly terrified of Scarlett's plans for their future. He was frantic to follow her to the ends of the world if that was what she would ask of him, but he knew without a fraction of a doubt, that he was compelled to release her and leave her to go on without him.

He had no desire to restrict Scarlett on her new journey to liberation; he was convinced that there was no place for someone like him around her. It enormously frightened Blade to release her, but at the same time, he was anxious to make the most of what was left of their time together.

Scarlett was immensely looking forward to Matthew's return while Lily had grown increasingly supportive and protective of Scarlett. She had stepped in on more occasions than one to defend her daughter against Pastor Joe, while his sermons focused to a greater extent on discipline at home and how imperative it was for his flock to seek repentance and absolution.

He would often refer to the tainted sheep that would wander off aimlessly and how imperative it was for the Shepherd to return his sheep to its natural surroundings. Scarlett would unintentionally glare at Pastor Joe during his sermons; she was no longer listening to his preaching. She no longer understood her father and she no longer lingered under his curse.

Scarlett sat on the Church benches and was no longer mesmerized by the way he spoke. She would drift off into her own little world and she would find Blade waiting there for her. She would escape into her world of magic and stars in a distinct effort to avoid the brunt and anger of her father.

When Scarlett walked out of the Church one Sunday morning, she looked up at the sky and realized that winter was in full swing. She knew that any day now, the snow would begin to fall while the icy flakes would cover their entire village. Scarlett adored the snow, but that year, she found the mere thought of fighting through the snow to reach Blade at the barn entirely disheartening.

When she met him at the barn that same night, she was saddened by the fact that he had left the graduation ceremony as suddenly as he did.

"I looked for you, but you were gone?" He placed his arms around her and held her firmly against him.

"I, I didn't want anyone to see me, but I am so proud of you, Scar. Scarlett Rose, high school valedictorian."

She sighed at the mere thought.

"Was it that bad?" He gazed questioningly at her.

"I am the Pastor's daughter, it is that bad."

They made their way around the back of the barn and sat at their usual spot.

"You have sand on your hands again!" She giggled as she

# The Weeping Prince & The Mansion in Sand

took his hands into hers.

"I miss the beach, but mama says that Matthew could take me the moment he comes home." She excitedly gushed as she smiled from ear to ear.

"You must be so excited."

"I am, Blade. I tell you, one of these days my sand castles are going to stand firm. The stars will light them up and you will see them from space." She burst out laughing while Blade gazed despondently at her.

"Why do you look so sad, Blade? What's the matter? Did something happen?"

At that very moment, he discovered something magic about Scarlett. She was unlike any other girl he had met before and her faith in the universe was infallible. Blade at once understood what her mother meant when she told Scarlett to be wonderful.

She already was, but Pastor Joe as dimming the light inside of her. He had fallen in love with Scarlett, and it scared him almost to death to realize that she loved him almost as much. She chose him; the boy from the wrong side of the tracks. Scarlett had willingly chosen to meet him in secret while she was abundantly aware of the history between the Bannisters and the Horaks.

He understood for the very first time that Scarlett Rose was entirely devoted to him, Blade Bannister; the boy she was warned against.

"You never ride your motorcycle anymore? I would love to ride with you again." She smiled as she recalled the very first night they met.

"I, I no longer have it."

"Why not? Blade? Why not? You love that motorcycle!"

"I just, I just don't need it anymore, Scar."

"Blade, that doesn't mean that you can't keep it?"

He turned to gaze up at the stars. She could at once sense melancholy in his eyes and was devastated that he had given up his motorcycle.

"I'm sorry you did that, Blade. I just don't understand why you did?"

"That's alright, Scar. I just no longer needed it. It's a long story."

"I'll be eighteen in three months, you know?"

"Yeah." He responded forlornly while Scarlett became increasingly confused by his morbidity.

"What's the matter with you tonight, Blade? Don't you want to be here?" She felt fear gripping at her heart by Blade's seeming reluctance to converse with her.

"We're supposed to be making plans for our future which is just around the corner. After all these months of meeting up in secret, we finally have a chance to go away together, and you don't want to talk to me?"

Blade noticed the tears in her eyes while he was keenly sensitive to the desperation in her voice.

"Scar, it's not that." He was frantic for Scarlett to understand that he was worlds apart from her.

"I love you, Scar. I would give anything to spend the rest of my life with you. I would run to the end of the worlds with you for a chance of a real life together. To love you, but ..." He paused to take in a deep breath. Scarlett was perturbed at once as she felt her entire world shattering around her.

"But what, Blade?"

The Weeping Prince & The Mansion in Sand

"We are from different worlds, Scarlett."

"I don't care! I'm from your world, Blade. I want to be in your world. I love you! You are home to me." She burst into tears before she buried her head into his chest. Blade held her firmly in his arms while his own heart had crushed at that very instant.

"I love you too, Scar." Blade Bannister laid her down on the grass and gazed longingly at her. He kissed her earnestly while Scarlett felt her body begin to tremble. He held her firmly in his arms as he kissed her longer.

"Make love to me." She whispered through her tears. Blade stared at her for a moment before he lovingly undressed her.

"I am here because of you, Scar, only you." He whispered hoarsely as his body began to explore hers. He craved her skin, her smell and her touch while she hunted him to make her his.

He held protectively onto Scarlett for a moment afterwards before he helped her to her feet.

"Are you, alright?" He cautiously questioned her as he seized her into his arms.

"I love you, Blade. Don't ever forget and please wait for

me. We're going to do this; we're going to get it right, you and me, but you must wait for me. Please Blade, we're almost there." She begged him as he tightened his hold over her.

"I love you, Scarlett Rose."

As she made her way back home, the first flakes of snow had begun to fall. Scarlett was overjoyed that the season had finally begun and was certain that it was a precursor from the stars above.

When she climbed into bed, she revived their night together and lay thinking of Blade and the emotions he had woken up inside of her. She hunted him. She craved his touch and into her soul, Scarlett Rose discovered that she had found the one whom her soul loves.

She laid thinking of the day that she could turn her back on Pastor Joe and ride off into the sunset with Blade Bannister. The secret plans she was making was entirely consuming her.

She was desperate to take Blade's hand, and leave Carmel far behind her. Even though she would dreadfully miss her mother and Matthew, Scarlet realized that it was a relatively small price to pay for her freedom.

Matthew arrived home scarcely two days before

Christmas, which according to Pastor Joe, was at the very last minute. Scarlett and Lily were delighted to have Matthew home, even Pastor Joe's gloominess could hardly diminish their spirits.

"Matty!" Scarlett ran into her brother's arms as he made his way up the path of the Horak home.

"Hey beautiful!" He seized her firmly into his arms and spun her around in extreme animation.

"I'm so glad you're home, Matty."

"So am I. How have you been, Scar?"

"Okay, I mean, you know Pastor Joe?"

"You're almost there, sissy." He hugged her tightly before he made his way indoors.

"Hello, my boy!" Lily was thrilled to have Matthew back home.

"You look a little skinny. Is everything okay with you?"

"Yes Ma'am. I am good."

"Don't call me Ma'am, Matty, its mama." Lily was adamant that her children drop the formalities around her. Matthew frowned nervously when he turned and gazed

# The Weeping Prince & The Mansion in Sand

questioningly at Scarlett.

"I'll tell you later." She whispered in his ear. When Pastor Joe walked in, he brushed past Matthew as he made his way to the basin.

"Hello Matthew." He hurriedly began scrubbing his hands. "You sure took your time to come home."

Matthew was irate at once while Scarlett and Lily stared at one another.

"I am here now, but I could always leave again." Matthew replied sardonically even though he was desperate to avoid a confrontation with his father.

"Do what you must." Pastor Joe turned to face Matthew and glared irately at him.

"Matthew's not going anywhere!" Lily interrupted at once.

"Feel free to leave, Joseph. You are not making strangers out of my children." Lily had become livid at once.

"Your children?"

"Yes, my children."

Pastor Joe slammed the towel onto the kitchen table before he stormed out of the kitchen.

Scarlett and Matthew glared tensely at one another as Lily picked up the towel and neatly folded it before letting out a faint giggle. Both Scarlett and Matthew giggled softly before they lovingly embraced their mother.

Carmel had turned into a wonderful picture-perfect Christmas village while Christmas trees and houses were decorated in anticipation of the Noel celebrations. Tourists had slowly, yet steadily made their way into Carmel while carolers were filling the streets day and night.

Christmas carols were heard echoing through the streets of Carmel and while people seemed more relaxed and at ease, Pastor Joe grew increasingly overwrought. Lily and Pastor Joe were barely speaking two words to one another, while Matthew and Scarlett noticed the mounting distance between them.

"I think mama's had enough of Pastor Joe." Scarlett whispered to Matthew one evening after dinner.

"Yeah, and about time too." Matthew responded with utter repugnance towards his father.

"Mama says he's been behaving extremely erratic

lately?"

"Yeah, nothing is right in his or the Church's eyes anymore." Scarlett responded in despondence.

"He wouldn't even give permission for a prom, but then again, he never allowed it before." Scarlett was at once accepting of the fact that he would in no way at all, alter or compromise any of his unyielding values.

"Yeah, even in my time it was taboo. I hope mama dumps his sorry ass."

Scarlett erupted into laughter as they sat out on the porch.

"So, sissy, what are your plans for the new year?"

Matthew was excited that Scarlett had finally completed her high school era. Scarlett smiled broadly as she turned to glance around her. She was cautious to keep her secret from Pastor Joe, afraid that he might act out in retaliation towards her mother.

"Father said something about a union between you and Carter Jethro? I assume he means that the two of you are going to be married? I hope you are not going through with it, Scar?"

Matthew was at once horrified and perturbed by the very impression.

"No Matty. Carter and I are friends, good friends. He's been my cover actually; my get out of the house card. He's actually seeing someone else on the sly, but you cannot tell anyone!" She giggled nervously as Matthew listened attentively to her.

"Oh right, I think? This is a little confusing?"

"He's seeing Jonas Walton, but please don't say anything, not even to mama!" Scarlett whispered almost inaudibly while Matthew glared in utter astonishment at Scarlett.

"What? He's gay?" Matthew erupted into a fit of laughter by the mere contemplation.

"Oh man, Pastor Joe would just die!"

Scarlett giggled nervously while continually glancing around her. "I'm, I'm leaving Carmel, Matty. Father doesn't know."

"You should Scar, but where will you go?"

"On the morning of my graduation, mama gave me an envelope …" Scarlett was nervous and fearful that Pastor Joe might eaves-drop on their conversation.

"She, she gave me money, Matty. Money that she had been saving and she told me to take it and leave Carmel after Christmas."

"Do it, Scar. Leave this village and never come back here."

She was at once thankful that Matthew supported her as abundantly as her mother did. She got up and placed her arms around her brother,

"Will you check in on mama, Matty?"

"Of course, I will, sissy, but you have to be careful out there in the world on your own. You can always come and live with me?"

"He'll find me if I run away to you, but, I, I won't be on my own, Matty, I've met someone."

"You have? Who?"

"Blade ... Blade Bannister."

"Can't say that I recognize the name?"

"Oh Matty, there is an age-old family feud that has been

lingering between the Horaks and the Bannisters for over two hundred years. Pastor Joe sent him away and treated him like a dog when he showed up here one night."

"A feud? I know nothing of an age-old feud?" Matthew was confused by all that Scarlett was revealing. She hurriedly told him about the two families and their farm lands. She informed Matthew of the devastating fire that had crippled the Bannister family. She told Matthew that she was convinced that the Horaks were responsible for the fire.

"And now, father says he comes from the wrong side of the tracks."

"What a bastard, Scar. Do you love him, sissy?"

"With all my heart, Matty. He is home to me. I love him so much, he is such a good man, Matty."

"Does he treat you well?" Matthew noticed her tears brimming in her eyes as she remained silent for a moment,

"My soul loves him, Matty and he loves me too. He takes care of me and he finds me. It doesn't matter where I am, he finds me."

"Does mama know?"

"No Matty, and you cannot tell her. She says she doesn't care, and that if Blade is the man I want, I have her blessing. It's just, what she doesn't know, can't force her to lie, you know?" Scarlett was desperate for Matthew to keep her secret.

"And you, big brother, have you met your match?" Scarlett was keen to discover whether Matthew had lost his heart to a woman just as she had to Blade.

Matthew lowered his head while shame had entirely engulfed him. "What's the matter, Matty?"

"Scar, listen to me. You can't tell anyone, not even mama, okay?"

"I won't, but you're scaring me?"

Matthew took her hands into his, as he leaned forward, "There is someone, and we, we actually got married in July."

"Oh Matty, that's wonderful! Why didn't you bring her home with you, big brother? I mean, what exactly could Pastor Joe do? And why haven't you told mama?"

"Scarlett, hush! Be quiet and listen! His name is Luke."

Scarlett gasped for air as her heart began to hammer ferociously. Her hands had begun to shudder as she understood what Matthew was telling her.

"You're, you're gay, Matty?"

Matthew once again bowed his head as he held her hands firmer. "Scar, please don't hate me. I didn't ask to feel that way about him, but I love him."

As he gazed into her eyes, she noticed a lost tear roll down his cheek. "I don't hate you, Matty. I don't care. I want you to be happy. I want wonderful for you and if you love him and he makes you happy, I have nothing more to say about this. I love you, Matty, but you should tell mama, at least."

"I can't tell her sissy. If she makes a mistake around Pastor Joe, he would be duty-bound to call an urgent Church meeting and expel that supposed demon from within...you know that, Scar? I can't do that to Luke."

"Yeah, I know, brother, it's just so unfair."

"So, will you take me to the beach tomorrow afternoon?"

Matthew frowned while gazing questioningly at Scarlett. "I'm not allowed to go on my own."

"What? Why not?"

Scarlett bowed her head as she began to tell Matthew how Pastor Joe had grounded her after the incident with Blade.

"Oh wow, Scar. Really? All of this because of an ancient feud?"

"Yeah, but it's not just that. According to Pastor Joe, he's below me and beneath the Horak family. He pitched up here one night, but Pastor Joe was having none of that and sent him away at once. He thinks he's left town."

"Oh man, what a corrupt man!" Matthew was horrified by his father's unexpected, yet erratic behavior.

"I'm so sorry Scar, I feel like I left you in the hands of a monster."

"It's alright, Matty. Mama stands up for me these days."

"Yeah, I heard, and according to the grapevine, you had an enormous meltdown in Church."

Scarlett smiled broadly as she told her brother about the humiliation she had brought into the Horak family. "I told him he was a hypocrite in front of the entire congregation."

"High five, sissy! You make me proud!" Matthew lifted his hand as Scarlett bumped his with her own.

"But, that's why I'm grounded, and that's why I am not allowed at the beach without a chaperone. I haven't been in months, so you just have to take me tomorrow!"

"Sure Scar, I would love to."

"Now, tell me more about Luke! When do I at least get to meet him? When did you know, Matty? I mean, I never guessed, not even once and not even while spending all that time with Carter and Jonas."

"I've always known, Scar. Since I was a little boy, I've known. I tried to fight it. I tried my best to like girls and to look at them in the same way I looked at boys, but I couldn't, sissy. I fell in love with Luke from the moment I saw him for the very first time."

"Oh Matty, I am so happy for you."

"Can you imagine Pastor Joe's reaction when he finds you gone and that his prodigal son likes men?"

They both burst out into laughter at the mere thought.

Alice VL – Zandri Burger

# PASTOR JOE'S MORTAL SIN

"Scar, wake up." Scarlett awoke to find Blade at the foot of her bed.

"Hey, what are you doing here? How did you get in?" She whispered while desperately afraid that Pastor Joe might find Blade in her bedroom.

"It's the day before Christmas; will you meet me at the barn tonight?" She sat straight up and gazed cynically at Blade.

"Yes, just try and stop me! I want more than anything to ring Christmas in with you."

"Shhh, your parents might hear you. See you tonight, all right?" He hurriedly kissed her on the cheek before he disappeared through her bedroom window. She smiled at the very thought of spending Christmas Eve alone with Blade.

Scarlett quickly made her way downstairs, and was pleased to find Matthew seated at the kitchen table.

"Morning, Matty." She kissed him on the forehead

before she took an empty seat beside him.

"Morning Scar and Matt." Her mother had groggily entered the kitchen shortly after Scarlett had taken her seat at the kitchen table.

"Where is Pastor Joe?" Matthew turned to face his mother.

"He is at Mr. O'Hara's house to lead a prayer. This reminds me, father has asked that you help out at the Church Fête today, Matt."

"But, I promised Scarlett I'd take her to the beach."

"Oh, that's okay, we're all going to the beach tonight for the fireworks display. We'll all go together tonight. Let's just not rock the boat on Christmas Eve."

Scarlett sighed as her disposition had instantly altered.

"I'm sorry sissy, but I promise you, you can stay as long as you want tonight. And I will take you tomorrow, and the day after, alright?"

"Sure Matty, thank you, brother."

"I'm surprised he allowed the fireworks display, mama.

What happened?"

Matthew was at once confused by his father's willingness to allow the display which he had turned down each year before. Lily shook her head as she poured herself a cup of coffee.

"I'm pretty sure he wants to preserve the little favor he has left by the town. What will you be doing today, Scarlett?"

"I don't know, mama?"

"Well, I do." She reached into her pocket and handed Scarlett a mobile phone.

"I received this phone in the mail, did you know that you can buy almost anything off the internet? Pastor Joe is to know nothing of this. Apparently, you can research anything on it, other than make or receive calls. You can even go onto the internet, and find all sorts of things. I thought you might need it to research your future plans, and of course, to call me once in a while. So today, you are going to find your tomorrow with this amazing little device." She smiled despondently at Lily before she got up to embrace her.

"Mama, thank you." Scarlett took Matthew's hand into hers as they strolled down to the beach just as the sun was about to set. Pastor Joe and Lily followed securely behind them while they noticed the gathering crowd excitedly anticipating the fireworks display which was due shortly after sun down.

They had barely reached the beach when Matthew noticed a crowd forming an anomalous circle. Scarlett and Matthew hurriedly made their way over to the horde and when Scarlett peered through, she gasped for air when she noticed a sand castle; one like she had never seen before. Scarlett stood staring in silence and when she peered closer, she realized that the tide had come in, but the crashing waves were powerless to wash the magnificent mansion of sand back into the ocean.

She stood staring at the perfect sand castle, and was instantly paralyzed while in awe of the magnificence that stood in front of her, in all its enchanting splendor. It had been built. Her sand castle was effortlessly withstanding the heavy gusts of winds that had suddenly surrounded them. As she watched in absolute amazement, the entire sand castle lit up, bit by bit.

The entire crowd gasped for air when they realized the phenomenon that was taking place right in front of them. It was beautiful and for Scarlett, it was a miracle, the miracle that she knew would find her.

"I wonder where the lights are coming from?" Matthew whispered as he stepped closer. "Probably just Christmas lights?"

The Weeping Prince & The Mansion in Sand

Scarlett stepped right up to the sand castle while entirely conquered by a sense of marvel and incredulity. She stared at it where it stood unyielding and lit brightly, in all its magnificence and grandeur.

"There are no Christmas lights, Matty." She grabbed her brother by his arm to pull him closer.

"Look." She whispered before Matthew strolled around the sand castle. He was at once staggered by the mystery of the lights that were shinging through each window opening, and every doorway of the sand castle.

"Its magic, Matthew, just like I said there would be someday, magic."

"There's no such thing, Scar, and don't let father hear you speak that way."

"Matty, its magic, I can feel it." Her mouth had hung open as she struggled to grasp the magnitude of what they were presented with.

After gazing in bewilderment for just a moment longer, she frenetically turned to Matthew. "I have to find him, Matty." She became hysterical at once.

"Who, Scar?" Matthew stared at her in utter confusion.

"Blade. He did this, I have to find him! I don't care what you tell Pastor Joe, I have to find him, Matthew. He did this for me, he is my weeping prince ..."

She hollered out to him as she ran up a different path and disappeared into the bushes.

"Matt, where's your sister?" Pastor Joe became frantic at once when he failed to detect Scarlett amongst the crowd. Matthew swiftly glanced around him before he turned back to Pastor Joe.

"I, I don't know, father?" Matthew lied in a desperate bid to conceal the truth from Pastor Joe.

"Matthew, where is your sister?" Pastor Joe instinctively knew that Matthew was deliberately veiling the truth from him.

"She, she went to find Blade, I think she said." Pastor Joe gasped for air when Matthew mentioned Blade Bannister's name.

"What do you mean, find him?" He was bewildered at once.

"She said that he did this, he built the sand castle?"

Matthew stood motionlessly while he frantically attempted to grasp the engineering issue surrounding the sand castle and the lighting.

"I must say father, I have no clue how he lit up this sand castle, and from a student engineer's point of view, it is practically impossible. Scarlett is right, it's magic, it has to be."

Scarlett Rose rushed through the streets of Carmel on foot in a desperate attempt to find Blade. It was far too early to find him at the barn; she was certain that he would be at work, and when she reached Long John Mackenzie's Garage, she was relieved to find Long John Mackenzie about to lock up for the night.

"Mr. Mackenzie!" She breathlessly yelled out to him.

"Yes?" He turned to face her while she stood in silence in front of him as she attempted to catch her breath.

"I am Scarlett Rose and I'm looking for Blade. Is he still here?" She glanced around and immediately noticed his motorcycle parked in the garage.

"Blade Bannister? No child, he isn't here." Long John Mackenzie stared at her in bewilderment.

"Where can I find him? I have to find him?" Scarlett was desperate to track Blade down.

"I have no idea, Scarlett Rose. To be honest, Blade took off a couple of months back, I haven't seen him since."

"He hasn't been at work? What do you mean? When did he leave? And why is his motorcycle still here?" Scarlett was horrified to discover that Long John had had no contact whatsoever with Blade, and she was utterly puzzled that he had left his beloved motorcycle behind.

"August? Somewhere in August. He must have left on foot? He left no note young lady. It's as though he just vanished."

"But, I saw him, just last night? And the sand castle?" Her tears had begun to shimmer in her eyes while she was desperate to comprehend all that Long John was telling her.

"The barn. I have to go!" She bellowed out to him as she turned to make her way out to the barn, on the cliff.

Pastor Joe stood motionlessly as though frozen in time at the mere notion that Scarlett had run off in search of Blade Bannister. It entirely confused him that she had become so incredibly desperate to find the boy he had banished from Carmel many months ago.

"Where did she go, Matthew?" His voice was shuddering as panic and fear had engulfed his entire body.

"Father, you can't hold her back like this. You have to let her go." Matthew was desperate to talk sense into his father when he witnessed the sudden wild, yet unexpected and terrifying expression in his father's eyes.

"Matt, what do you know about all this?"

"I, she's been meeting him at the old Bannister barn on the cliff." Matthew was devastated for unintentionally exposing her secret.

"Blade? She's been meeting the Bannister boy? How? It can't be? Are you sure it's the Bannister boy?"

"Yeah, Blade Bannister? Father, let her be, please." Matthew made one last valiant attempt to save his sister from his father's rage and resentment.

Pastor Joe hurriedly turned away and found his way up the path towards the old Bannister barn on the cliff by the river, in a desperate attempt to uncover his daughter's secret.

When Scarlett reached the barn, she hurriedly made her way out to the back where she would habitually meet Blade night after night.

"Blade!" She was relieved to find him standing at the edge while he stood inertly gazing out over the ocean.

"Blade?" She whispered as she moved closer to him. When she touched his arm, he turned around to face her. He seized her into his arms and held her firmly against him. By the way he was holding her; Scarlett instantly sensed that he was dissimilar. By the expression on his face, she was convinced that he might be holding her for the very last time.

"Blade, what's the matter? You're scaring me." She retreated slowly as she gazed into his eyes.

"Scar ..." He began to choke on his words while his tears were rolling disconsolately from his eyes.

"Blade?" Scarlett pulled him closer and held him firmly against her, desperately afraid of letting him go. "I found the sand castle. It's too strong for the tide. You did it. You did it! It's magnificent, its magic, Blade. How did you do it? How did you light it up?" She whispered as she held him tighter. Blade remained silent as his tears were beginning to soak into her hair.

Scarlett retreated once again before she took his face into her hands. "What's going on, Blade? Long John says you haven't been at work since August? I don't understand what's going on? I saw your motorcycle, it's still there?"

She was desperate to understand Blade's abrupt disappearance and unanticipated anguish.

He retreated slightly from her before he took her hands into his, "I, I have to go, Scar. I have to leave here, you. I'm not from this world, Scar. I shouldn't be here. I don't know why I stayed, or how it was even possible, but I lingered, for you."

Scarlett was horrified by the mere thought of Blade's unexpected departure. "Go where? Don't leave me here without you, Blade. We can leave tonight, just you and I. We can run away together, and go far, far away."

She had become tearful almost at once. He walked over to the spot directly behind the barn where they had sat down countless nights together. When he reached the precise spot, he turned to face Scarlett one more time. "I was here for you, Scar. I stayed only for you. I couldn't leave you before, Scarlett. At first, I didn't know why, you know? I was so confused. I should have left that night. I didn't know what was happening to me, or … I just didn't know anything."

"Pastor Joe can't make you leave, Blade!"

"Nothing about this is right, Scar. I shouldn't be here."

"Blade! I don't understand what you are saying! You are scaring me! We have plans. We have a life waiting for us. We can be together!  Tonight, after tonight, we'll be together, forever!" Scarlett hollered through her tears that were bucketing from her eyes. "I love you, Blade. I don't, I can't live without you. You said you loved me!"

He lowered his head, pausing to take in a deep breath. Scarlett had remained stock-still as she desperately attempted to make sense of what he was saying.

"Scarlett Rose, I love you so much. More than life itself and I think, I think that that's why I am still here. I don't want to leave you, I just don't know how to stay here with you. Below my feet, here beneath me, Scar, this is where you will find me. This is where I am. This is where I really am. None of this is real. None of this matters. Nothing is as it should be. Below my feet, Scar, you will find my bones right here, here where Pastor Joe buried me."

At that very moment, Scarlett gasped for breath before a bright light had begun to encircle him. "What? What are you saying?"

Scarlett had erupted into tears as fear had begun to overwhelm her. "I don't, I don't understand! What are you saying, Blade? Your bones? Pastor Joe buried you? What are you talking about?" She hollered out desperately through her agonizing tears, utterly frantic to hear him tell her that what she had heard, was wrong.

"Do you remember that night when I pitched up at your house ... uninvited?"

"Yes?" Her voice had begun to shudder uncontrollably.

"Pastor Joe, your father struck me down that night."

"He struck you down?"

"Scarlett, your father murdered me that night and then, then he just buried me here."

"No Blade, that can't be. It can't! Then, how can you be here? How can I feel you? How can I see you? How did I meet you here night after night? How did we, no Blade! No! You are not dead! You are here! With me! I see you! I feel you!"

"I don't know, Scar. I don't have the answers, but I do know that I was real because of you."

"I don't believe you! If you want to leave, then just tell

me! Don't stand there and tell me that you're dead when I can see you, and feel you!"

Blade moved closer to Scarlett and as he reached out to hold her in his arms, she abruptly retreated from him.

"Stop lying to me! Just tell me that you don't love me!" Scarlett felt her entire world collapse around her. She could barely breathe as she felt her heart shattering into a million pieces.

"I love you! I don't want to leave you! I love, love you, Scarlett, and I am so sorry. I don't understand any of this myself, but I am so, so sorry."

"Blade! Stop! Just stop!" She shouted out as she swiftly ran into the barn where she found a shovel, the only implement in the entire barn. She hurriedly made her way back to the very spot he was standing on, before she frantically began to dig into the ground as her heart had continued to shatter into a thousand more fractions.

She had been fiercely digging for what felt like forever when she struck what she thought was a rock. She tossed the shovel to one side while she frantically attempted to wipe the sand from the solid object beneath her with her bare hands. Her hands were shuddering while her heart was pounding. She was desperate to discover that all he was telling her was a lie.

Scarlett stood back in horror when she discovered a partial skeleton, a frame of bones that once belonged to another human being. The bones that Blade Bannister was claiming belonged to him. She fell to her knees before she covered her face with her hands, sobbing violently into them.

Her heart could no longer survive the anguish. Her body ached all over, and the little voice inside of her became silent, while the pounding of her heart had almost come to an abrupt halt.

"Scarlett Rose! Scarlett!"

She faintly heard Pastor Joe's voice from a distance. As he was calling out to her, his voice became louder and clearer. Scarlett knew that he was fast approaching her, and when she turned to find Blade, he could be nowhere to be seen.

When Pastor Joe reached her, he was at once unprepared for, and horrified by her unexpected discovery. She stood glaring at him while her tears were pouring hopelessly from her eyes. She shook uncontrollably, while the restricting lump in her throat mercifully silenced her.

"Scarlett?"

He whispered croakily as she stood over the remains of the man she loved. The man she had spent night after night with, yet the same man that perished on the very second night of their meeting. Blade Bannister had habitually met her at the exact spot his body was laid to rest, while he listened to her make plans for a future and a life together.

At once, she understood why Long John Mackenzie had never again heard from Blade since the night he showed up at her door. She finally understood why he left his motorcycle behind, and with utter shock and overwhelming devastation, she realized why her father was so awfully frantic to scrub his hands as vigorously as he did when he returned from his walk with Blade.

"You did this? You murdered him! You stole the only man I would ever love from me! You have his blood on your hands, father!" She managed to utter almost inaudibly while unreserved fear and devastation had delimited her.

"It, it was an accident, Scar." Pastor Joe lowered his head in dishonor.

"What happened? Tell me what happened? Tell me! How

did it come to this! How could you? How was it an accident? Joseph Horak! You tell me tonight!" She shouted out to him through her endless supply of tears.

Pastor Joe hesitated before he gazed fearfully into her forlorn eyes. "I, we went for a walk. All I wanted was for him to leave you alone, with the family feud and all. But, he wouldn't listen, Scar. He refused to stop seeing you. I just wanted to protect you from him, from his name."

His voice was shuddering ferociously as he began to tell her the story of how he murdered the man she loved far than she had loved herself.

"Protect me from him? He was the only one that ever truly loved me! And then, father? And then?" She shouted once again.

"I struck him, Scar. He fell to the ground. He must have knocked his head on something. He stopped breathing. I tried to revive him, but I couldn't. I didn't mean to slay him. I swear Scar, it was an accident. It was a terrible accident." Pastor Joe had burst into tears while confessing his mortal sin.

"I brought him up here and I, I laid him to rest. I didn't know what else to do?"

"You laid him to rest? You didn't lay him to rest! You dumped and hid his body! If it was an accident, why didn't you notify the authorities? Why did you bury him out here, hoping that no-one would ever find him?"

"I don't know, Scar, I don't know?" He covered his face with his hands one more time while desolation had crept up, and overwhelmed his entire body.

"May God forgive you, Pastor Joe, because I never will! Not only have the Horak family destroyed the Bannister family, but you have single-handedly ended the life of the last living Bannister, a Bannister that I loved! A Bannister that I wanted to spend the rest of my life with! You have the entire Bannister family's blood on your hands! God will never forgive you for this. I will never forgive you for this! Never! I loved him so much. He came back father, for me. Each day, he came back for me! He was here because of me! Night after night, I snuck out of the house and met him here! He built that sand castle on the beach, you know? The one that was lit up? He did that! He came back …"

She speedily ran up to the edge of the cliff before she turned to face her father one more time. "You took everything from me. I have lived my entire life to please you. You were my hero, daddy. You were the one that I once felt safest with. I loved you! I idolized you! And the one time, the one time I wanted to follow my heart, you imprisoned me! When I fell in love, Pastor Joe, you punished me for it! All I wanted was for you to trust me and support me. I never asked anything else of you. Never, father, never."

She whispered hoarsely as she gazed at her father through the devastation and darkness that had entirely encompassed her. She was instantly aware of a shadow beside her, and when she turned to look, she discovered Blade standing next to her.

Scarlett smiled sorrowfully at him while utterly relieved that he had returned to her. "I am so sorry, Blade. I get it now. I choose you, Blade Bannister."

Pastor Joe gazed questioningly at her, uncertain of whom it was Scarlett was talking to. "Take me with you. You are home to me. I don't want to live here without you. I love you." She whispered hoarsely as she reached out for him.

"Scarlett?" Scarlett turned to find Matthew when she heard his voice when he appeared beside her father. He at once noticed the shallow grave that had been dug up. He glared incredulously at Pastor Joe, before he grimaced and gazed over at Scarlett.

"Pastor Joe killed him, Matty. He killed him. He murdered him!" Scarlett cried out in desolation as her brother stood motionlessly, unable to understand the sequence of events that had unfolded only moments before.

Matthew stared at her in disbelief before he glared cynically at his father. Pastor Joe lowered his head while overcome with sorrow and indignity. "What is she talking about?"

Matthew was desperate to understand what it was that had so enormously devastated Scarlett.

"Matty, tell mama she was a wonderful mother. Tell her that I love her. Please tell mama that I am so thankful for everything. Matty, you have to notify the authorities. Pastor Joe must be punished for this. Free mama from him, Matty. Promise me, you will free mama from him? Tell the towns folk of Carmel all that Pastor Joe had done, don't leave anything out, and then, Matty, you tell them about the Bannister fire. You tell them everything, Matty! You must restore the Bannister name, brother. You must tell the truth. Please, do this for me, please, Matty. Make things right for the Bannisters, my brother. They didn't deserve any of this." She begged her brother while desperate for him to give her his word.

"Scar?" Matthew was at once terrifyingly aware that Scarlett was saying goodbye. He was desperate to reach her, afraid that she might jump.

"Matty, step back. Don't come closer. Just swear to me, please? I have to know that you'll do this for me." She pleaded with him once more.

"Scar, I promise you, I'll set things straight. I will tell the world what Pastor Joe has done, but don't do this. Please Scar, I am begging you. We will notify the authorities together, sissy. We'll take mama, and we'll leave Carmel. Pastor Joe will rot in jail until the end of time, and then God will take it from there. Scar, please don't do this. This isn't what Blade would want you to do. Don't do this to me, Scar, I am begging you." Matthew was pleading through the tears that had begun to roll down his own cheeks.

"I can't, Matty. I can't stay here without him. My heart will not go on. Be wonderful, Matty. I love you. I only wish, I only wish I had met him ... Luke."

"Scarlett Rose, please don't. I will hand myself over. You are committing a mortal sin by taking your own life." Pastor Joe was desperate to bring Scarlett Rose back to him.

"Like father, like daughter." She whispered.

"You did this, father. This is all you. You have distorted my soul and tainted what is left of my life. I have no life without Blade. I love him. He came back for me. We are unfinished, father, and I don't want to live the rest of my life without him. I am not the first Horak to die here, Pastor Joe, but I pray to be the last. I know all about Catherine Horak. I know about the fire, I know it all. I know everything …"

Scarlett had become calm and spoke gently. Her heart was no longer hammering, and the restricting lump in her throat had disappeared.

"He's home to me, Matty, and I want to go home." She was desperate for Matthew to be aware of the fact that she had no life without Blade.

Scarlett reached out for Blade's hand, and when he clutched hers into his, Pastor Joe and Matthew were susceptible to a bright light that had surrounded the silhouette of a man standing beside Scarlett Rose.

"Goodbye Matty, I love you, big brother. Please take care of mama. Don't let her cry. Tell her that I will be near her, always. Tell her, tell her that just as Blade stayed close to me, I will stay close to her. Please don't let her cry for me. I am happy now. Tell mama that this is what I want. I choose him, tell mama that. Tell her that I am happy now." She whispered contentedly before she abruptly flung herself off the cliff, while holding firmly onto Blade's hand.

From a distance, she could hear her brother calling out to her. She looked up, and noticed the fireworks that were lighting up the entire sky in Carmel. Scarlett smiled, and when she turned, she saw Blade right beside her.

As she was falling the hundreds and hundreds of meters to the river, she thought about her mother, Lily. She reflected back to a time when she was only a little girl. She recalled how her mother affectionately nursed her when she would become ill. She thought about the countless of band aids she would place on her knees and elbows.

She pondered back to a time when Lily would devotedly brush out her hair, and adoringly braid them for her. She could in no way quite consider when it was that she had surrendered herself to Pastor Joe and his rules, and then she recalled the night that her mother had released herself from his hold. She smiled as she remembered her mother's eyes, and she at once was certain that she could feel her mother's arms around her.

The Weeping Prince & The Mansion in Sand

"I love you, mama."

Scarlett's mind drifted back to her brother, Matthew. Her pillar. Her support structure. The only one she could safely share her secrets and heart's desires with.

She recalled back to a time that he would pick her up after she had fallen, and how he would carry her into their home while demanding that her mother patch her up, and mend her wounds. She thought back to the hundreds of moments that they would hide in the garage where they had discovered an old radio, and where they would tune in to listen to the Top 100 countdown each Saturday night.

In an instant, she could see his smiling face in front of her. She felt safe again.

"I love you, big brother."

Scarlett thought back to Pastor Joe and his undeniable cruelty. She could by no means at all think of one day that she felt loved and cared for by him. She thought of herself as a soldier while he was the commanding officer.

She was at once distraught by the notion that she had continuously engaged in a courageous effort to remain the perfect daughter for him, one he would be proud of, and one he might love someday. She could by no means reflect on one moment that she witnessed his laughter, or even a smile. His eyes had remained lifeless almost throughout her entire life.

Scarlett closed her eyes before a broad smile formed around her mouth. She was tired. It was time to go home.

Alice VL – Zandri Burger

The Weeping Prince & The Mansion in Sand

When Scarlett opened her eyes, she was surrounded by a million tiny, white lights. She cautiously turned around, and was at once pleased to find Blade standing behind her.

"Where are we?" She whispered while instantly aware that her feet felt as light as a feather, and that her heart no longer ached. The anxiety and fear that had surrounded her earlier, had made way for feelings of exhilaration and relief.

"You have found forever, Scar. We're amongst the stars." He whispered gently as he took her hand. "I want to show you something."

He vigilantly led her up a ladder that had reached the millions of stars, and while they climbed on every one, he turned and pointed, "Look."

Scarlett was thrilled to discover that the sand castle on the beach was undoubtedly visible from where they were standing. It had stood firm, and it had stood tall, just as she once imagined it would. The light radiating from inside the sand castle was almost blinding, and when she turned back to Blade, he could witness uncontaminated enchantment in her eyes.

"It's beautiful."

"Would you dance with me, here amongst the stars?"

Alice VL – Zandri Burger

The Weeping Prince & The Mansion in Sand

He held his hand out to her.

"I would love to."

She took his hands into hers, and gently squeezed them. As she placed her arms around him, she heard the faint sounds of crashing waves. She held him firmly against her as they began to dance.

When she glanced down at the sand castle one more time, she noticed with sadness that the light was beginning to dim. She stared at it in a desperate attempt to memorize her sand castle, afraid that she might soon forget.

She gazed deferentially at the sand castle, until the light had wholly died out while the brutal waves had crashed unsympathetically into their sand castle, effortlessly destroying it in one foul flounce until it was entirely returned to the sea, almost as thought it was never there.

Blade & Scarlett-Rose, looking down on you.

## THE END

Alice VL – Zandri Burger